` J
. Jones
  Edge of two
  worlds

C   A

Kern County Library

1. Books may be kept until last due date on card in this pocket.

2. A fine will be charged on each book which is not returned by date due.

3. All injuries to books beyond reasonable wear and all losses shall be made good to the satisfaction of the librarian.

4. Each borrower is held responsible for all books borrowed by him and for all fines accruing on them.

DEMCO

Edge of Two Worlds

Weyman Jones

Edge

# of Two Worlds

Illustrated by J. C. Kocsis

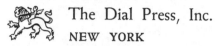

The Dial Press, Inc.
NEW YORK

Also by Weyman Jones

THE TALKING LEAF

To Marilyn

CONTENTS

Edge of Two Worlds

ONE

Alone

THE ONLY living things in the whole stretched-out and sun-burned world of Texas seemed to be Calvin and the yellow grasshoppers. He hadn't seen a jackrabbit since yesterday morning, and now not even a buzzard teetered in the empty sky. Just grasshoppers. They buzzed out from under every step he took, flailing their double wings, only to crash sprawled and scrambling in the white dust.

Calvin was tired, and beyond that. He was not walking anymore. Instead, he thought of his right foot, lifted it carefully past his left and put it down. Then he leaned on it, thought about his left foot, lifted that past his right and put it down. Between each step he paused to gather himself for the next.

He often fell. Sometimes he lay in the hot dirt a long time, watching the grasshoppers.

The lump on his head and the bruise on his side where he had been thrown against the wagon seat didn't hurt anymore. He didn't even feel his blistered feet and sun-burned neck much now. When he hauled himself up to his knees and then staggered back to his feet, it was like moving underwater, pushing against something.

He wasn't hungry anymore either. Yesterday when he crossed a muddy creek, he had caught three minnows and a tadpole with his hands. The minnows he ate raw, but the tadpole was so soft and squashy he couldn't put it in his mouth. After a few miles more he had decided that throwing the tadpole back had been silly. It was more like something to eat than grasshoppers.

But that was yesterday. Today he didn't care about anything.

Whenever he looked around, the edges of the prairie rushed away into the hard blue sky on all sides, leaving him in the empty middle. Looking back, he could see only his last two or three footprints, so quickly did the dry wire grass spring back, leaving no trace of Calvin.

Everything was the same: the same toast-brown tufts of grass, the same yellow-freckled boulders with the same heat halo shimmering above them, even the same grasshopper flying heavy curves ahead and then waiting for him, staring solemnly from the underside of a ragweed leaf. He knew better, but he felt that this was the same grasshopper he had first seen hours and miles ago this morning, or yester-day—how many days had there been?

How long had he been standing now, staring at the idiot

face of the yellow grasshopper swaying on a stalk and dribbling a bubble of tobacco juice?

He tried again, a dry croak: "Hello! Help!"

The emptiness swallowed his voice without an echo. The prairie air, like the wire grass, seemed to push back in its own way, so that his voice probably reached no deeper into that stillness than the trace of his last footprint in the rising grass behind him.

When he looked back, the grasshopper was gone, but Calvin could still see it, real as a face in a fever dream.

Big yellow eyes. The Indian had painted two yellow circles like bug eyes across his forehead and under his cheekbones, and his face had been as expressionless as the grasshopper's as he went from one teamster to the next where they lay scattered around the broken wagons, still as dolls. The Indian carried a rifle but he didn't use it. Just the knife.

Once when he was little, Calvin had fallen into a dry well behind the corral. He stepped back against the edge of the cover, felt it give and skid, and then his foot went into nothing. He bumped twice against crumbling walls and landed on his back in damp sand. He seemed to be looking up through a funnel. The dirt walls seemed to lean toward him, shrinking the bright disk of the well mouth while he chewed at the air, trying to get enough inside him to cry.

Afterward his father asked if he had seen the stars. "You can see 'em in broad daylight from the bottom of a well," he said. Calvin nodded as if he had noticed.

He sat on the split-rail fence and watched his father haul rocks to fill the dry well. After that he never was especially afraid of the place. But there was always a well inside him where his nightmares lived. Some nights he could feel the lid stirring when he slipped into sleep and then, if he was lucky, he sat up in bed and slammed it back. He used to cry when he was little. Later he just sat up and looked around his room under the ranch house eaves, naming the furniture shapes until he made everything familiar again and the lid was back on the well.

Sometimes he wasn't lucky enough to wake up in time, and then the lid came off and he dreamed.

Now Calvin tried to slam the lid down on the Indian again. The Indian wasn't a dream, although Calvin kept thinking of him that way to keep the lid on his memory.

He should have stayed there in the weeds where he had landed when the wagon tipped over. He could have hidden until the Indians left, then followed the wagon tracks back to the river, and then he could have made some kind of a raft and drifted downstream until he came to a ranch or a town.

He should have stayed hidden—but how could anyone stay and watch? When the seven Indians slipped off their painted war ponies and started going from one to the other of the three teamsters who lay in the wreckage of the wagons, Calvin had crawled away.

But not before he saw what they were doing. Now he wished he had gone sooner, so that he wouldn't have that picture in his nightmare well: the knives glittering, the blood—

so much blood, like a butchering back home—and worst of all the bug-painted Indian who found Joseph, the lead teamster, still alive and not far from where Calvin was hiding.

When the Indian turned away, carrying Joseph's scalp and leaving a red horror in the weeds, Calvin crawled down the little draw until it flattened out into the prairie. He crawled into the open, never looking back, on and on until he wore out the knees of his pants and then the skin off his knees. When he finally stood up, feeling tall and conspicuous, and circled back, he couldn't find the tracks.

He had walked all day, hoping to come to the river over each rise, but it was never there. By the time he realized that he didn't know which way the river was, he didn't know which way the wrecked wagon train was either.

When it got dark, he lay down in the dirt. He kept sliding off toward sleep until he felt the cover lifting on the nightmare well, and then he would jerk awake and try to think about the river. But sleep finally tricked him. He woke up screaming and scrabbling in the dust, with the morning sun in his face.

That was this morning. Today he was just walking, pressing down with the full weight of his mind on the well cover.

Nothing was as bad as remembering that. Not being lost. Not even knowing that he would never get home again. Nothing. And so Calvin thought about nothing except not thinking about the Indian. Soon he would be too tired to lift his feet anymore and past caring altogether, and then he would stop, and after a while he would be a clean white bone grinning at the sun.

Calvin looked around, trying to get the lid down. A feather of smoke seemed to rise through the heat-wiggling prairie air and disappear. He wiped his sleeve across his eyes and squinted, looking hard into the throbbing blue nothingness. Not even a wisp of a cloud. He knew the smoke hadn't really been there, but he turned that way, thought about his right foot, lifted it past his left, and started again.

If it had been real, it might be the buffalo hunters.

That gave him something to think about. Last week, sitting in the wagon bed, he had watched the dust puff turn into a single stretched-out spot, to three shapes, and then to two horses with riders followed by a white pack mule. One of the buffalo hunters had a yellow moustache, he remembered. That night they had all camped together, and Calvin had gone to sleep listening to campfire yarns. The next morning he had watched the hunters shrink into a spot again and finally disappear in the west.

Could that smoke mean they had found game and made camp here? A grasshopper sailed past Calvin's ear and rattled into a wind-polished boulder ahead, scrambled up and cocked his legs under him. Calvin thought of the Indian again and stopped. Smoke could mean the war party too.

Nothing moved. After a while Calvin heard the rattle of grasshopper wings once, and then silence again. There was no more smoke. Had he really seen it? Nothing seemed real except the heat and the dust.

He took off his hat to shade his eyes, blinked and

squinted, looking hard. No smoke, but something. A shadow, or a swale of grass? No—a line of trees.

He started walking toward them. Now he didn't have to think about each step.

At first the trees seemed to get closer. Then for a long time they seemed to keep their distance, walking in step with him across the prairie. There was no more smoke, and by the time he reached the first stunted and twisted oaks, he was sure there had never really been any.

But he still tried to walk quietly, although his feet seemed far away and the ground kept coming up to meet them so that they stumbled along on their own, cracking the woody stalks of dried weeds. Calvin couldn't make himself care much. He seemed to be watching everything from some place nearby, and as he got closer to the trees, he even whispered advice to himself.

"Get down," he said, and he did, onto his hands and sore knees, trying to crawl through the weeds without moving them. When he crawled into the ragged edge of broken shade, the well cover inside him lifted once and he thought of the Indian. He pressed it back by saying, half out loud, "The smoke wasn't real. It wasn't ever really there." He looked around and picked up a smooth rock the size of an ax head and crawled on.

A woodpecker hammered. A honeybee blundered around his poppy-red neck. There—was that running water? Before he could be sure, he came out onto the crumbling edge of the riverbank.

The river was real. It was mostly sandbars and it looked

wading-deep all the way across, but the steep banks showed that it ran higher sometimes. Cottonwoods grew along the edge, roots sticking out in places where high water had washed the dirt away from their grasp.

Calvin wanted to belly flop into that cool wetness but he hesitated, looking at every rock for a sign of scorch and wrinkling his nose as he sniffed for any hint of smoke. Nothing. He had known that all along, really.

He stood up, but still he hesitated. His back and shoulders ached from so much crawling, and so he leaned against the peeling trunk of a big sycamore and looked around. Just being away from the grasshoppers among trees that shut out most of the sky gave him a safe indoors feeling. In a moment he could splash into the water. He rested his head against the tree, closed his eyes and took a deep, slow breath.

A man coughed—quietly—very close.

Calvin jumped away from the tree. The rock dropped out of his hand, tumbled down the bank and splashed into the water. He looked around—dead into the eyes of the Indian.

TWO

The Cave

CALVIN'S EYES locked into the Indian's. Neither moved. Calvin could see a third eye below the Indian's, looking at his stomach. It was the muzzle of a rifle. Calvin knew this little steel eye was the last thing he would ever see, and so he kept looking into it, as if his eyes could hold the bullet back. The moment stretched out and finally snapped, and Calvin looked up at the Indian. Those eyes were as black as the rifle's.

Slowly the idea grew in Calvin that the Indian was not going to shoot. He hadn't shot Joseph and the other teamsters. Not after the attack, when he had Joseph helpless like this. The Indian had used his knife while Joseph was still alive.

Then another idea struggled slowly into shape: this wasn't the same Indian.

He didn't wear a scalp lock. Instead, some kind of red-

and-yellow cloth was wrapped around his head like a turban. Instead of a loincloth and vest of dyed quills, he wore a blousy shirt of something like curtain cotton, open at the neck where a silver chain glinted, baggy at the elbows and belted with some sort of shiny blue sash.

Calvin started to breathe again. Where had he seen clothes like those before? Somewhere, he couldn't remember—but it had nothing to do with Indians.

The man was standing on something below the riverbank, his head level with Calvin's boot tops and the rifle angled across the crumbling edge of the bank. Where had he come from?

Very slowly Calvin tried one step back. The man twitched the rifle and made a noise. It was not a word, but it was a sound Calvin had heard before, and he stopped. Sweat tickled down his back. Another bee buzzed and stopped, buzzed and stopped somewhere.

Nothing moved. The fever-dream feeling settled over everything again.

Now he remembered: turban, tunic and sash—this dream Indian was mixed up with the pictures of Moses and Abraham in the fat Bible Mother kept on the round table in the parlor. Just as Calvin was trying to tell himself that maybe this wasn't even an Indian, the man motioned with the barrel of the rifle and said something, the bitten-off grunt as before, and now Calvin remembered. It was what the grasshopper-painted Indian had said when he took Joseph's scalp. The sound of it now made Calvin remember how Joseph had cried out, once.

Calvin started backing away, but the *crick-crack-crick* of the rifle being cocked stopped him. The Indian raised the rifle to his shoulder. Calvin knew there were worse things than a bullet, but the rifle was *now* and he stopped.

The Indian motioned again, and Calvin took a step forward. The Indian nodded, and Calvin took another. One more, and he was at the edge of the bank. The Indian squatted and backed into the mouth of a cave that Calvin could see now under the sycamore.

The tree was keeping a wedge-shaped piece of the bank from washing away. Sometime when the water had been higher, it had tunneled a shortcut behind the fist of roots, and the Indian was sitting on his heels now in the mouth of that cave. He made a downward motion with the rifle.

Calvin hesitated. The Indian raised the rifle again, and Calvin edged down the slippery bank, stepping carefully to avoid any sudden off-balance jerk.

The Indian thumbed the hammer back to half cock and squat-stepped deeper into the little room carved by the river, as Calvin came down. When Calvin stood in the mouth of the cave the Indian was sitting on his heels in the other entrance on the downstream side.

Calvin looked around. The river licked the bank just below his bootheels, and from here it looked deeper. How far could he swim underwater?

The Indian made that bitten-off sound again, and Calvin looked back into the eye of the rifle. He stooped and took one step inside, shoulders against the gravelly mouth of the cave. Suddenly his knees began to shake, as if they had

just realized that this was really happening, and he sat down on the damp clay.

Now he could see that the Indian's face was textured with tiny wrinkles, and again he thought of the family Bible with its worn calfskin binding. Had he ever heard of an Indian living in a cave? This one was very old, and Calvin had heard of burial mounds and dressing up the dead in their fanciest clothes for the trip to the spirit world. Maybe this one had been left here to die.

He seemed to be waiting for *something*.

Finally Calvin swallowed twice and said, "Do you speak English?"

The Indian didn't move.

"If you help me get home, my father will give you money."

Nothing. Did he ever blink?

Through the pattern of Bible-cover wrinkles, deep creases ran from each corner of the Indian's mouth to make a V where they met the lines from either side of his nose. Even the squint wrinkles in the corners of his eyes seemed to point down, as did the corners of his mouth and his nose, high-bridged and pinched at the tip like an arrowhead.

Calvin looked at the rifle muzzle again. Did the Indians take prisoners with them to the spirit world? He couldn't remember.

He looked around the cave. Wool blankets spread at the back. Saddlebags against the wall, showing fancy silver buckles with a monogram, and next to them a narrow book with leather corners like the ledger where his father kept the ranch records—plunder, obviously, from some other white travelers. Two bundles hung from a stake driven into the wall of the cave, wrapped in what looked like uncured deerskin, hair side out. Meat, perhaps? On the other side a tiny fire glowed in the nest of roots, and he noticed that a chimney hole had been cut alongside the sycamore trunk so that whatever smoke escaped would be scattered by the leaves. Out on the prairie he must have been looking at just the right moment to see it.

"My father will pay you," he said. "My father is an important man in Texas. A lawyer. He used to be a judge back in Missouri. He owns a white house and a lot of land. . . ."

The Indian just sat there.

Moving slowly, eyes on the rifle, Calvin emptied his pockets onto the floor of the cave.

"Here—I have sixty dollars of American money. You can have it."

The Indian didn't move.

"Here—look at this. This is my father's watch. Look here—see my father's name on the back? It's kind of rubbed off now, but you can still read it. Or you could if you could read. See—Calvin Harper. That's my name too. Take it. You can have it."

The Indian didn't move.

Calvin leaned back against the dirt bank and put his head in his hands. He was tired, tired. So tired.

"Calvin Harper," he said again, just to hear the sound of his own name.

After a while a noise brought him back from somewhere, not from sleep but from some gray place past caring. He raised his head. The Indian was standing, holding the rifle. Calvin glanced toward the mouth of the cave and moved his feet under him, but the Indian stepped out the back entrance to the cave and climbed down to the water's edge.

Calvin could see a hole the size of a small pail dug in the riverbank there, with water standing almost to the top. The Indian knelt and drank. When he finished he climbed back into the cave and motioned to Calvin.

Calvin crawled past him through the little tunnel and then half slid on his heels down the bank. The hole was lined with pebbles that filtered the river water as it seeped in.

He had forgotten how thirsty he was. He drank the little well almost empty, and then he sat down on the bank and took off his boots. He stripped off his socks like corn husks and then dangled his feet into the soupy water. He filled his hat and poured the water over his head and sunburned neck. When the filter well refilled he drank it down almost to the bottom again.

He climbed back into the cave, carrying his boots and putting his sore feet down carefully on the gravelly clay. The Indian had unwrapped one of the deerskins, and he handed Calvin a strip of dark meat.

His stomach started to ache, waiting for it to get down, but it was so dry and tough it took a lot of chewing. As he ate he nodded and smiled at the Indian, who didn't eat. He looked at the other parcel at the back of the cave. It was as big as a quarter of beef. This Indian had prepared for a long trip to the spirit world.

Feeling brighter now, he decided to try again. He pulled on his boots, forced a big smile and stood up, stooped over in the low cave. The Indian didn't move.

"Thank you. Thank you for the food," he said, mouthing his words as if he were talking to a deaf man. "I'm going now, but thank you." He started a step back.

Before his heel touched, the Indian had whipped the rifle away from the wall of the cave, levered a round into the chamber, and pointed the little steel eye at Calvin's belt buckle.

Calvin teetered and then brought his foot back. "Why don't you let me go?" The Indian didn't move. "What use am I to you? All I want to do is just go home."

The Indian thumbed a left-handed gesture toward the ground, and Calvin slumped down again. The Indian eased the hammer down to half cock and leaned the rifle back against the wall.

Calvin could hear thunder muttering. Green flies buzzed around the deerskin parcels in the back of the cave, and something—a carp, probably—slurped at the top of the water below them. The Indian coughed again.

Calvin put his head in his hands again and started sliding back toward that gray place past caring. The thought lazed through his mind, without any feeling, that no one would ever know what had happened to him. He wondered if his father would put up a stone in the family cemetery on the little hill behind the springhouse. He could see it:

CALVIN HARPER
1827–1842
Beloved Son

Last summer Calvin had carved his initials in the walnut tree where the swing hung over the creek, and now he wished he had carved his full name.

"Calvin Harper," he said out loud.

"Where is your camp?" the Indian said.

For a moment the words didn't reach Calvin in his gray place, and then he jerked his head up. He opened his mouth to answer, but his tongue stuck to the roof of his mouth. Had the Indian really spoken English? Or were his ears playing the same tired-tricks that his eyes had played on the prairie?

The Indian wiped his forehead with the back of his hand, and Calvin noticed that the old man's face was shining with sweat. "I know you didn't come alone," the Indian said. "Where are the others?"

Calvin had to clear his throat twice to get any sound out. "They are dead," he said. "Your—the Indians killed them."

"What kind of Indians?" the old man asked.

"I don't know—Indians."

"Just Indians," the old man said.

The cave filled up with silence. Finally Calvin said, "Why don't you let me go?"

"Because I don't believe you," the old man said. "I'm not sure that you don't have a camp somewhere around here. Maybe you just wandered away and got lost. Maybe if I let you go you would find your way back and tell them about an old Indian hiding in a cave."

"What if I did?" Calvin asked.

"There are white men who collect the ears of Indians. Just any Indians. They string them on sticks."

The Indian began to shiver. Without getting up, he reached behind him and gathered one of the blankets around his shoulders. Calvin remembered that a little earlier the Indian had been sweating. Chills and fever.

"I'm telling the truth," Calvin said. "I don't know what kind of Indians they were—Apaches probably—but they attacked our wagons and they killed the drivers. I got away because I don't think they saw me. I was sitting down in the bed of the wagon behind the seat, and when the wagon tipped over I was thrown out into some high weeds. Anyway, I got away. But they're all dead. I watched the Indians I know they're dead now."

"If I let you go, you'd die too," the Indian said, his teeth rattling slightly with the chill. "An Indian boy could live on this prairie, but you'd die."

"I could make it," Calvin said. "Please, just let me go."

The Indian pulled the blanket closer around his shoulders, and Calvin realized that the sunlight was no longer reaching through the front entrance of the cave. In the silence the thunder grumbled, closer now.

"Where are you going?" the Indian asked.

"I was going east," Calvin said, his words stumbling over each other. "I was going to a place in the East called Boston, where there is a big school. My father wanted me to go there to study the laws of the United States. He believes that Texas will soon be a part of the United States. I thought I wanted to be a lawyer—like my father."

"But now you're just going back home?"

"Now if I can just get home I won't ever go past Snake Creek again."

The Indian was looking beyond him at something outside. Calvin turned and looked, but he saw only the riverbank.

"Twice today I have seen a honeybee," the old man said.

Calvin nodded. He remembered a bee in the woods when he was crawling in to the riverbank.

"What did the Indians look like?" the man asked.

"One of them had yellow paint on his face. In circles, like bug eyes."

"Feathers?"

Calvin nodded.

"Up or down?"

"What do you mean?"

"Did they wear the feathers pointing up or down?"

Calvin hesitated. "I don't remember. I only got a good look at one of them."

"What did they carry—rifles, bows or lances?"

"Rifles. And they rode like—I never saw such riding. They came down the slope zigzagging and making their horses rear every time they switched back, prancing and showing off. And then when they came into range, they dropped over the side and shot out from under their horses' necks."

"Comanche," the Indian said. "They braid rope loops into their ponies' manes. A Comanche can hang on with one heel on his pony's back and his elbow in the loop, so that he has both hands for his rifle. There it is again."

"What?"

"The bee. I want some honey."

"Honey?" Calvin asked.

The Indian nodded. "I'm too sick to eat this smoked deer meat. The honey would stay in my belly. If I let you go, you could follow those bees to the bee tree. But I don't think you would come back."

"Yes, I will," Calvin said.

"You are all great promisers," the Indian said.

He reached into a crevice in the wall behind him, brought out an iron-headed tomahawk and tossed it beside Calvin. "Here," he said. "Follow the honeybees. It is late in the day now. They will be going back to the bee tree." He paused for a moment. "Did you ever rob a bee tree?"

Calvin nodded. The Indian looked at him—into him, it seemed—and Calvin was sure that the lie showed.

"Do you have matches?"

Calvin fumbled in his shirt pocket and brought out the little tin box. The Indian nodded. "Go on then," he said. "But remember those Comanche. A little smoke shows a long way out here. Just use enough to quiet the bees. A bee sting is better than a scalping knife."

Calvin stood up, bent over in the low cave. "I'll remember," he said. "I don't want to see any more Comanche."

Without moving a muscle in his face the Indian reached

out and grabbed the nape of Calvin's neck, jerking him forward, off balance and so close that the fever heat of the old man's eyes held him fixed.

"You don't want to see any more Comanche," the old man said softly. "What do you really want, boy?"

"I just want to go home."

"You can't do that. You can't do what you really want. But you're going to have to decide what to do." He let go, and Calvin jerked up so suddenly that he staggered backward.

"Remember, I have meat," the Indian said. "This is a big hungry prairie. You'll be all alone again, while you decide. You'll have to decide whether you're more afraid of an old man, who doesn't wear paint or feathers, or whether you're more afraid of the prairie. Being alone on the prairie."

Calvin nodded and took another step. The Indian made a flicking gesture, and then he bit off that sound again, the sound the grasshopper-painted Indian had made as he reached for the teamster with his knife. Calvin kept his eye on the rifle as he backed out of the cave.

THREE

The Storm

CALVIN CLIMBED carefully up the slippery riverbank. Keeping his eyes on his feet, he walked through the big trees close to the river into the bushy thicket of scrub oaks. He didn't hurry or look around. He heard nothing behind him, but he was sure the Indian had followed him out of the cave. He was probably standing again with the rifle angled across the bank, and Calvin could feel the exact spot between his shoulders where the eye of the rifle was looking. That was just how the Indian might do it—tell him he was letting him go and then shoot him down as he walked away. That would be an Indian idea of fun, a joke. This close, would he hear the sound of the shot?

The sapling scrub oaks were all around him now, and he let his feet hurry a little. He wanted to look back to see if the Indian was following, but he kept his eyes on the squared-off toes of his boots. He counted fifteen steps, and then he was out in the dry weeds. He looked up. Ahead was a low rise. He walked toward that, a little faster now in spite of himself.

Going over the top of the rise was the worst moment. If the Indian was going to shoot, it would be now.

And then he was running down the far slope, running until his side hurt, looking back over his shoulder now and then to see the scrub oaks grow smaller behind him, then jumping and skipping, until finally he slowed to a walk. After a long time he stopped and sat down against a rock. He fanned with his hat and laughed out loud.

A gray lizard scuttled out from under the rock, saw Calvin and stopped.

"Hello, Horny," Calvin said, trying to laugh again to stop the tears that were running down his face like the last time he had really cried, when he was just a kid.

The lizard looked at Calvin with one eye and did push-ups. Calvin couldn't stop sniffling, and after a while he quit trying. After all, he was alone.

Alone. He raised his head and looked around. The lizard was gone, but there was a yellow grasshopper staring at him from a swaying sourweed stalk.

Calvin stood up and kicked at the grasshopper. It sailed away ahead of his boot as if it had heard what he was thinking. He climbed on top of the boulder and looked around. Now that he knew the river was there, he could see that the wiggle of trees across the prairie obviously traced its course. But just where was the cave?

He would wait until nightfall and then work his way well below. Did he know for sure which way the river flowed? Yes, it was to the left. He looked up at the sun, now only a pale smudge in the thunderheads piling up overhead. The river flowed south and east. Home was probably due west. But that didn't matter. The river would eventually take him to some white settlement.

He sat down against the rock again. His father said that changes in weather bring out the worst in animals, the way whiskey does in Indians. When a storm is coming, dogs turn coward and cringe under the porch, horses pitch and cows hook. "And," he always finished, "kids turn sillier."

Calvin waited. He heard a meadowlark call. Something stirred the grass nearby—a field mouse, or perhaps a blacksnake. A bee sailed into the timothy grass around the edge of the boulder, buzzing from clump to clump, looking for blossoms. The water and the strip of smoked meat had awakened Calvin's hunger.

Would anyone ever believe he had been held prisoner by an Indian dressed like Moses? And that the Indian had actually let him go?

Or even that an Indian could speak English like a schoolteacher? Looking back at it, the Indian had hardly seemed scary. More like an old man than an Indian.

He watched the bee, remembering what the Indian had said: "This is a big hungry prairie." He touched the tomahawk at his belt. A honeycomb would keep him going for days. He looked at the sun, almost snuffed out by clouds. Only an hour or two before sundown.

He hesitated. He didn't like the thought of going back into those trees anywhere close to the Indian's cave. But the thought of the honey, thick and dark with waxy pieces of the broken comb mixed with it, tasted so good in his mind that his jaws ached.

He stood up, but the bee didn't go anyplace. It bumbled from one tiny clump of yellowish grass to another as if it had discovered a field of sunflowers. Twice it started across the prairie but each time it circled back. The thunderheads mumbled to each other, and Calvin looked up. The flat-bottomed clouds seemed to sit on top of the air, the way mountains must look to a fish through the top of the water. And then, as if his thought of water had started something, he felt a drop on his ear. There was a pause. The wind sighed again and then raindrops thudded around him, each dimpling the dust like an ant lion's trap.

Calvin looked around to find the bee again. He walked a spiral, kicking the weeds as he passed, but it was gone.

Lightning rip-crashed nearby with a glare of light that seemed to be everywhere at once. Calvin smelled burned air. The rain and the wind stopped. The prairie seemed to hold its breath, waiting.

He looked around for cover. The prairie rolled evenly away as far as he could see, warted occasionally with wind-scoured rocks. He looked at the trees along the river. That was the worst place to go, he knew. Tall trees draw lightning, and tornadoes follow the lowest land, which would be the river bottom.

And besides, the river was where the Indian waited.

Even as he was telling himself those things, alone on the open prairie waiting for the storm to break, the shelter of the trees looked inviting. He found a rock that had one sloping face. With the tomahawk he hacked out the dirt under it until he could sit in a little hole with the boulder hanging slightly over him.

Back home, even the cattle had range shelters. Most of them were just brushwood roofs over open hay ricks, but they were better than this.

The storm began gently as a garden rain. Then three shots of lightning broke open the sky. Rain puddled in the dry dust. Thunder cannonaded across the prairie, and between the cracks the wind sobbed. Calvin shivered in the muddy hole with water whipping his face. The afternoon went abruptly into twilight.

Finally he crawled out from under the rock, stood up and peered around, looking for the wobbling tail of a tornado, but it was raining too hard to see anything.

Rain coursed off the top of the rock in a solid stream, filling the hole he had dug. A twisting fire-snake blasted out of the sky, so close it seared his eyes, and actually bounced off the prairie in front of him. Calvin ran toward the trees, slip-slopping across the spongy ground, until another flash showed empty prairie ahead. Where were the trees?

Just then a giant insect wing wrapped around his face and stuck, wet and filmy, across his nose and mouth. He clawed at it, blind and breathless in the driving dark. Some of it tore loose in his hands, and a lightning flash let him see it. Tumbleweed.

He stood still, scrubbing his face with his sleeve until his shuddering stopped, and then he looked around, waiting for another flash. When it came it showed empty prairie ahead.

He faced around to the left and waited again. Empty prairie that way too. He turned some more and waited. The next bolt seemed to show something, but he couldn't be sure. Again—was it the dark line of the trees? He started walking that way. After a long time he felt the first scrub oak saplings switch his legs.

Under the trees it was dark and dripping. He found a wind-felled tree still full of leaves, crawled under the trunk and lay down, shivering, on the wet ground. After a while, in spite of everything, he slept.

In his dream, a huge yellow grasshopper chased him across the prairie. He ran past a well, and somehow it was the one behind the corral at home. The lid moved and water gushed out, flooding the prairie under his feet until he was struggling through a rolling ocean. The grasshopper bounded along the wave tops easily, but Calvin floundered into deeper and deeper water. First it was over his feet, then his knees, and then, when the water reached his waist, the grasshopper caught him, slapping a wet, filmy wing across his face.

Calvin awoke. He was lying in water. He knew the grasshopper had been a dream, but when he looked around he saw water everywhere, and then he thought perhaps he was not yet awake. There was a noise—running water. The river.

Calvin sat up and bumped his head against the tree trunk. He scrambled out and stood up, blinking in the pale early daylight. All around him the trees were standing in muddy water. He rubbed the bump on his head, trying to understand.

There was no sign of the riverbank. The river had overflowed all the way to the first growth of stunted trees at the edge of the prairie. It must be running through the Indian's cave, top to bottom.

"He probably didn't get out at all," Calvin said, out loud. "And even if he did, he couldn't last through that night. Not sick with fever, and old as Moses to start with." Had the horny lizard drowned too?

He was just as alone and lost as before, but everything seemed different now. Instead of the sun and the empty prairie there was a fine mist and a muddy river. He had eaten yesterday and now he was hungry again. Instead of thinking about the Indian, Calvin started looking around for driftwood and thinking about how to make a raft without nails or even rope.

This river might even take him right back to Snake Creek. He could see the muddy shallows where he had caught crawdads for fishbait on other summer days, and imagine squishing wet-booted up the cow path past the swing hanging over the water-drop. Shep would come down from the corral, barking at first but wagging all over when he recognized Calvin, and then his father and mother, standing in the door of the springhouse, maybe—he could even smell the cool, buttery springhouse breath—and he would never leave again. Not for college, not for anything.

And he thought again of the old man in the cave, wondering if he had gotten out.

He walked along the edge of the brown water until he came to a little rise where the ground was solid under his boots, and then he sat down. After a while the rain stopped. He took off his clothes, wrung them out, put them back on—shivering at the clammy feel of the damp cotton—and sat down against the tree again.

A spider labored to fix the wet ruin of yesterday's web in a low branch, and Calvin thought about running down the cow path on summer mornings when beads of dew sparkled in the corn-spider webs spun overnight across the path. Some were always stretched so high that he wondered how the spider got the first strand across.

He thought about his mother and father. For some reason he could not call up their faces clearly. What would they be doing now? Finishing chores, or maybe at breakfast. Would they be talking about him?

After a while he slept, jerking uncomfortably awake from time to time and then drifting dully back. When the sun came out he opened his eyes and stared up at the leaves for a long time, thinking nothing. The spider had finished the new web. Then he sat up, wrinkling his nose. Woodsmoke.

FOUR

The Bee Tree

THE BREEZE shifted and took with it the whiff of wood-smoke. But he had smelled it, he was sure. He turned his head slowly, hand on the tomahawk in his belt. A flicker whipped from branch to branch overhead, his motion doubled by the reflection in the muddy water. Nothing else moved.

Maybe a lightning bolt had started a smoldering fire in a dead tree. It couldn't be the Indian. Calvin tried that out loud: "It can't be the Indian."

He rolled onto his hands and knees and crawled away from the trees into the prairie until the ragweed and wire grass were tall enough to hide him. Then he sat up and looked back.

The rain had beaten down the grass in muddy swirls on the half-bald ridges of the low hills. Among the trees along the river, bark-stripped scars showed where the wind had twisted off limbs. Broken clouds scudded low over the treetops.

The corners of his eyes picked it up first—a gray streak rising close to the place he had been sleeping. The breeze off the rain clouds was scattering the smoke before it rose to the tops of the trees, so that he couldn't see just where it started.

Running stooped over to stay close to the tops of the weeds, Calvin circled well upstream, slipped into the timber as far as the water line, and then walked back carefully from tree to tree, the tomahawk in his hand.

After a long time he smelled smoke again. He stopped behind a huge oak, wiped the sweat-slippery handle of his tomahawk, and then picked out a trail to the next tree before he started. The grass was wet and limp, so that, jumping over the wind-felled branches, he ran without a sound.

At the next tree he heard something like the rasp of two limbs rubbing together on a windy night. The smell of smoke was strong now. Ahead was a hickory standing almost in the water. He could see the butt of a fallen limb sticking through the low crotch, about twice as high as his head. Calvin ran light-footed to it and peeked around the trunk. He saw nothing except the leafy branches of the fallen limb. As he looked around it to pick out his next tree, the leaves moved. Calvin stepped away from the trunk, looked up and saw the Indian.

He was lying flat along the slanted limb, which he was

using as a ladder to climb up to the crotch of the hickory.
Calvin couldn't see his face, but he recognized the red-and-
yellow turban. He stepped quietly back to the tree and
pressed against it. The Indian was high enough to see
through the crotch, but he couldn't look straight down
the other side where Calvin was standing. Calvin glanced
around to pick out the best way to run.

There, leaning against the trunk, was the Indian's rifle.
Calvin risked one more quick look up. The Indian had
climbed all the way to the crotch now. Calvin took a deep
breath and picked up the rifle.

He backed away from the tree and then circled around.
He cracked the breech to be sure there was a round in the
chamber, and then he cocked the hammer with his thumb.
The Indian heard that and looked down.

He was holding a curved slab of punky stump wood, with
a fire smoldering in it. The Indian looked at Calvin for a
long moment and then, just as if he didn't see the rifle, he
turned back to the tree. He rested one corner of the burning
slab in the crotch of the tree and began to blow on it.

Calvin took a step back so that he could see what the
Indian was doing. The tree was hollow at the crotch, with
a long hole running up the inside of one of the big limbs
like a slitted eye. The Indian was blowing smoke into it.
An occasional bee flew out, staggering through the smoke.

Calvin tucked the rifle into his shoulder and tried to
steady the sights on a place just above the Indian's blue
sash. The rifle seemed suddenly heavy, and the front sight
kept tracking back and forth across the Indian's wet shirt.

He tried to see the war-painted bug face in his mind's eye, but instead he noticed how the curtain-cotton shirt clung to the Indian's frail shoulders.

Just then the Indian looked around. Calvin could see that his face was wet with fever sweat again.

"Remember the ears," the Indian said. "An Indian's ears will bring a dollar in San Antonio."

The Indian's eyes held Calvin's the way they had when he first looked into them. The drunken buzzing of the bees seemed to grow louder.

"Did you decide to come back, or did the storm decide for you? People have always decided for you, haven't they, boy? Now you're at the edge of a decision."

The rifle seemed so heavy that Calvin lowered it, just for a moment, so that he could hold it steady.

The Indian turned back and blew some more smoke out of the smoldering punk. Calvin shifted the rifle in his hands, watching.

A bee stung Calvin on the back of the neck. He jerked and slapped at the spot, holding the rifle in one hand as he took a step backward.

The Indian said, "If you're not going to shoot, then throw me the hatchet. Unless you want to chop this honey out yourself."

Honey. Calvin could see it glistening through the smoke. He remembered how it looked at home, black in the comb but amber on biscuits, flecked with pieces of wax. Why not? He had the rifle.

Calvin lowered the rifle butt to the ground, pulled the

tomahawk out of his belt and tossed it up head first. The Indian caught it with his left hand.

Holding the burning wood carefully with one hand, he began to chop out sections of the bee tree. Smoke-dopey bees boiled out, flying crazy circles and landing all over the Indian. Some of them must be stinging, Calvin knew, but the Indian worked methodically.

After a while he dropped the tomahawk and cut the main section of the comb loose with his knife. Then he began to stack the three chopped-out pieces of tree trunk with the comb hanging from them, balancing the one big lobe of free comb on top.

Calvin brushed his fingers across the sore spot on his neck until he could feel the stinger, and then he pulled it out. When pieces of bark pattered on the ground, he looked up. The Indian was coming down.

Calvin grabbed the tomahawk from under the tree and shoved it into his belt. He stepped back as the Indian straddled his way carefully down the limb without dropping the honey and sat down cross-legged against the tree. He held out one of the chunks of wood.

Calvin took it with his right hand, holding the rifle in his left.

The honey was waxy and thick, so sweet it set his teeth on edge. He ate it all and then licked the rough wood. The Indian ate a little and put the rest aside. He poked some mud loose with his knife and began to smear it on the places where the bees had stung him. After a while he stood up and said, "Give me the rifle."

Calvin shook his head and took a step back. "No," he said. "I'll keep it."

He swung the muzzle around toward the Indian and took another step. The Indian stood still, looking at him. In the silence, Calvin could hear the angry buzzing of the bees. He cleared his throat and pitched his voice low, hoping it would come out deep and manly. "I'll keep the rifle," he said.

The Indian smiled a little and nodded. "All right," he said. "Then shake it out."

Calvin hesitated. "Go on," the Indian said, "shake it."

Calvin turned the muzzle down and shook the rifle up and down. Something rattled. A piece of wood showed at the muzzle, and Calvin pulled it out. It was half as long as the rifle, shaved to fit snugly inside the barrel.

The Indian said, "When I had to leave my rifle to climb the bee tree, I fixed it to blow up in the face of anyone who fired it." He smiled. "In case the Comanche are still around."

Calvin looked down at the shaved stick. It was trembling now, and he dropped it.

The Indian walked to a clump of high weeds where his blanket roll was hidden. "Here," he said, "eat some meat. We have a long way to go and I don't want you to hold us up."

Calvin backed away. "Go where? I'm not going anywhere with you."

The Indian rolled up his blankets, tying the ends with rawhide. "Where *are* you going, boy?"

"Home. I'm going to make a raft and float down the river until I get to some place where there are people. People who'll help me get home."

The Indian shrugged the blanket roll over one shoulder. "Did you ever make a raft?"

Calvin didn't answer.

"I'm going to make a raft too. Probably tomorrow. I'm going to cross this river and then I'll be finished with the raft."

"Why don't you cross here?" asked Calvin.

"Here the river goes the way I want to go and so I can follow it a ways. Where it turns, the river will probably be narrower and easier to cross." He licked a smear of honey off the back of one hand and made a gesture with his head, pointing downstream with his chin. "Come on."

Calvin shook his head. "I'll make my own raft."

The Indian studied him a moment and then said, "You know this is Comanche country. Sometimes the Comanche hang a white prisoner head down over a small fire and watch him jump and wiggle while his brains cook."

Calvin took another step back, holding the rifle in both hands. The Indian twisted a tiny downward smile as he went on, "But I am Cherokee, and we have never broken treaties with the Comanche, or stolen their children to sell as slaves, or slaughtered the buffalo so the Comanche had to eat snakes and mice and finally their own horses in the winter. The Comanche may let you keep your hair if you are traveling with me."

FIVE

Comanche Country

WHERE THE sunburn had peeled off Calvin's neck the tender new skin was burning again. The wet foliage breathed clouds of stinging gnats into his face. Horseflies bit through his shirt. Mosquitoes welted his wrists. He limped, trying to stay off the blister on his right foot, and he noticed that the Indian limped too.

Twice Calvin had asked, "Where are you going?" But the Indian didn't answer. He looked yellowish and sick. He ate a little honey as he walked but he never stopped, and when Calvin lagged behind, the Indian speared him with a look that made him hurry to catch up.

As he trailed along Calvin tried to remember what he knew about Indians. He had heard of Cherokee, but he had never seen any. He had seen the little bands of Caddo and Wichetaw that stopped to water their horses at the Snake

Creek crossing below the south pasture. They were silent, dusty people. They used a few grunt-grumbling words that his father said sounded like a man chopping wood and wading upstream at the same time, and even their gestures were Indian.

He knew they had other ways of talking to each other—hand signs and signals of smoke in the daytime, and burning arrows at night.

When the Indian finally stopped for a moment, he didn't have to say anything. He just pointed with his chin, Indian fashion, raising his eyebrows, and Calvin understood as clearly as if he had said, "Aren't the rifle and the hatchet getting heavy? Don't you want me to carry one of them?"

Calvin shook his head and they went on. Later, when the Indian paused for him to catch up, Calvin could almost hear him say, "Come along, if you're coming. Surely you can keep up with an old sick Indian who was left by his tribe to die."

But Calvin kept falling behind. Once, without realizing it, he let the Indian get out of sight in the brush. Calvin stopped and looked around. He had the hatchet and the rifle. The river had scattered driftwood all along the banks. He could run back the other way until he came to a big log, shove it out into the current, straddle it and then float downstream until the Indian was far behind. He could float all night, just to be sure. Then he could make a raft somehow and drift until he came to a ranch or maybe even a town.

Calvin hesitated. Nothing moved around him. The shrill-

ing of a cicada overhead began to seem louder. And then
louder, as if the bug were coming closer. Louder. Calvin
looked up. On a low branch crouched a grasshopper, looking back at him. Bug eyes, Comanche yellow. Calvin ran
to catch up.

All afternoon they followed the river, walking just at the
edge of the trees, sometimes ankle-deep in water. Calvin
noticed that whenever they came to a rise the Indian went
a little deeper into the trees, so that he was in heavy cover,
and then paused on the top to look around.

What would his father do if he were here? Calvin began
to talk to his father, at first in his mind, then under his
breath and then out loud.

"You always told me the most important thing, if I'm
lost, is pick a way to go and stay with it." Saying the
words he could see his father nod, squeezing his bottom lip
between his thumb and forefinger the way he did when he
listened to arguments in court. "You said, 'Don't get milling
around in circles and then quit. If your horse seems to
know where he's going, let him go. Or if you've got a dog,
stay with him.' That's what you said. Well, this Indian's
going somewhere. Right now he's going downstream, and
that's the way I want to go too."

Out loud it didn't sound very convincing. He could
imagine his father's left eyebrow going up as he listened,
and stumbling along in the brushy river bottom, Calvin felt
his neck flush with embarrassment. He tried to hang on to
the feeling, because the embarrassment made it seem that
he really might get back home and need an explanation.

"Sure he's an Indian, but I have the rifle, don't I? I never let him get behind me, do I? And it might be true, what he says about the Comanche letting me keep my hair if I'm with him."

As he walked Calvin tried to find words to explain being alone on the prairie with the wire grass and even the air pushing back at him, and the way this old man talked English and looked like someone out of the Bible, not like an Indian at all.

Later that afternoon Calvin caught up with the Indian, sitting on his heels at the edge of a muddy slough where the river spilled into the prairie, looking over the water. Weed tops poked through the surface in places, and water spiders skated around the edge. Calvin sat down and fanned himself with his hat.

After a while the Indian pointed with his chin. "There—do you see him?"

"What?" Calvin asked.

"Fish," the old man said. "The overflow washed him up into here but now the river has gone down and he's caught. There—do you see him?"

The water boiled, and a forked tail flopped out of the water under a flooded tree about as far away as Calvin could have skipped a flat stone.

"It looks like a catfish," Calvin said.

The Indian nodded. "Go get him," he said.

Calvin stood up and started wading out to the tree. After three or four steps the water spilled over his boot tops, and Calvin stopped. He looked back. The Indian was still sitting on his heels, watching, as if waiting to see how long it would take Calvin to realize that he couldn't wade out, grope around in the water to catch the fish and then wade back while carrying the rifle.

Calvin stood knee-deep in the muddy water a moment, and then he splashed back up to the bank. "You go," he said.

The Indian looked at him and smiled, turning the corners of his mouth down, rather than up, as if he were smiling at something while smiling at himself for smiling at something in the first place. "I have the honey," he said.

Calvin sat down in the weeds and emptied his boots. "I'm not going," he said.

The Indian stood up. "Give me the hatchet then," he said. Calvin hesitated and then handed it to him, handle first, keeping a tight hold on the rifle with his right hand.

The Indian walked back along the bank to a clump of willows. He cut a sapling and walked back, stripping off the small branches as he came. When he reached the water's edge, he shoved the tomahawk into his own belt with a glance at Calvin and waded into the slough, probing ahead with the willow staff. In one place the water reached his waist, but under the tree it was less than knee-deep. He crowded the fish against the trunk with his legs and then picked him out of the water carefully, avoiding the stinging fins behind the gills. The fish was mud-gray on top and yellow underneath, half as long as the Indian's arm.

When the Indian waded back and dropped the fish in the grass, Calvin said, "I'll look for some firewood."

The Indian shook his head. "We have some more trail to make today," he said. "This kind of fish will stay alive a long time. Wrap him in wet leaves and he will still be fresh when we make camp tonight."

Calvin looked around. Fleshy pokeweed dangled limp and bedraggled in the shallow water. He picked some of the broadest leaves and splashed back to where the Indian sat on his heels, looking across the prairie into the sun.

"What's the hurry?" Calvin said as he plastered wet leaves around the pulsing fish.

"I have a long way to go, and not much time."

"Where are you going?"

"Don't worry about that, boy. Stay with me a while, and you will get to your school of laws."

"I just want to get home. And you're not headed that way."

"No. I'm not headed that way. You can't go back to being a boy with me." He snapped off a forked willow shoot. "Here, slip this through his gills. You can carry him."

Stumbling, sometimes staggering along, the catfish flopping against his legs as he hurried to catch up, the thought occurred to Calvin that maybe the Indian wasn't so old as he looked. Among the Indians, smallpox and even measles were terrible diseases. Perhaps there were others that would age a man's face but leave his body young, so that he could go mile after endless mile like this without stopping.

Just then the Indian stopped. He slipped off the blanket roll and sat on his heels. Calvin dropped the fish into shallow water and then sprawled on his back. Immediately he was asleep.

When the moccasin dug into his ribs, Calvin rolled over, clutching the rifle, broken sleep pounding in his head. "Don't kick me, Indian."

The Indian nodded. "Maybe you'll make it, after all."

"What do you mean?"

"When you're sleepy you talk like a man. Maybe you won't have to go home, after all." He slipped the blanket roll across one shoulder. "Come on."

The Indian didn't stop again until night was thick under the trees.

Calvin was following so blindly that he almost stumbled over the Indian stretched out on the ground with his head on the blanket roll.

Calvin stood a moment, knees trembling with fatigue, looking down at the Indian who lay still as death, and then he fumbled around in the dark until he found some dry wood.

He needed three matches from his tin box to get a flame started. As it pushed the darkness back, Calvin could see that the Indian was awake, watching him. He piled wood on the careless bright fire, but the Indian didn't say anything.

The catfish was stiff but still fresh. Calvin used the Indian's knife to skin it while the fire burned down. He latticed green branches across the coals, cooked the fish and offered some to the Indian. He shook his head, and so Calvin ate it all.

It tasted a little muddy, but it was rich and moist, not like the dry deer meat, and it felt warm in his stomach as he licked his sticky fingers.

The Indian stood up painfully, handed one blanket to Calvin and spread the other near the fire. He sat down again, moving in careful stages as if he had to send separate messages to his arms and legs. Calvin lay down on the other side of the fire.

After a while the Indian ate some honey. Then he raked a charred stick out of the fire and, propped up on one elbow, opened the leather-bound ledger book and began marking in it with the charcoal. Calvin tried to remember whether he had ever heard of Indians using picture signs.

The firelight glinted on the silver chain around the Indian's neck. Calvin thought of the watch in the snap-open gold case that his mother wore sometimes on a chain, and he wondered what was at the end of the chain inside the Indian's blousy hunting shirt, and how he had gotten it. A locket, maybe, from some white woman, perhaps with the miniature pictures of her children still inside. Calvin wondered where this Indian carried his scalps.

After a while the Indian closed the book and rolled up in the blanket as he turned on his back. He ate a strip of the deer meat, chewing it slowly for a long time with his eyes closed.

Then he seemed to sleep. A branch dropped in the fire and blazed up, lighting the Indian's face. He looked dead now. His mouth had dropped open and white showed between his eyelids. Scraps of hair had escaped from the turban, and they moved gently across his forehead in

the night breeze. Calvin thought again of Moses and
Abraham.

A coyote howled, and the Indian opened his eyes. He
turned over on his side, propped himself up on an elbow
again and reached into a fold of his blanket.

"Here," he said. "You left your watch and your money
in the cave. I had to leave my saddlebags when the water
came up, but I got out with half the meat and everything
I could roll in the blankets." He lay down again. "Since you
like to carry the rifle, you'd better carry your own money.
You can carry that blanket you're using too. We have a lot
of trail to make tomorrow."

"Where are you going?" Calvin asked. When the Indian
answered his voice sounded low and soft, as if it came from
far away.

"That way," he said, making a little gesture that somehow suggested a long distance. "Toward the land of the
black man. Where the sun goes down."

Calvin fumbled with words in his head, trying to find a
way to ask what he was wondering. Finally he blurted,
"What do you mean about the 'black man'? Are you traveling to the west, or do you mean toward . . . to your
own . . ."

"Death?" the Indian said. "That's who the black man is,
yes. And he's probably waiting for me there. But I don't
have to look for him."

"Why, then? I mean, where are you going?"

"I told you—where the sun goes down. To the west and
the south."

"But where?"

"You call it Mexico."

"Mexico? Why, that's—"

"A long way. And I have already come a long way. That's why I cannot take time to wait for you on the trail."

"Why are you taking me with you?"

The Indian raised himself carefully onto one elbow. "An old Indian traveling alone looking for his people doesn't

have to worry much about the Comanche," he said. "The Tewockenees, maybe. But they hunt horses more than scalps, and they've already stolen our horses."

"What do you mean, *our* horses? How many Cherokee are around here?"

The Indian didn't answer. Instead, he went on, "But the whites—white hunters, soldiers, and even the white ranchers—I worry about them. Maybe I'm a little safer traveling with you."

He turned over with his back to the fire, put his head on his elbow and went to sleep.

Calvin tried to get the rifle under his arm in such a way that the Indian couldn't slip it out after he fell asleep. He drifted off and then jerked awake, dreaming he had felt the

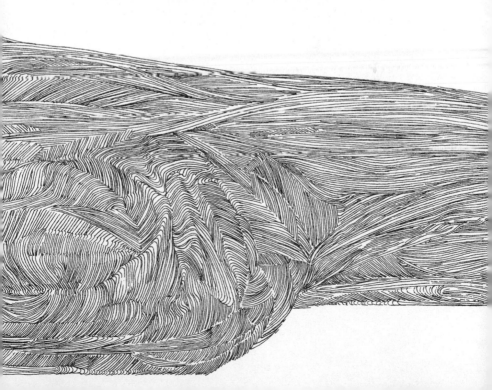

rifle move. The Indian was still asleep on the other side of the fire, which now was a heap of coals dusted with gray ash.

Calvin listened to the night rustles and calls. Each tree frog piped its own pitch. He could count five different voices for sure, with three other possibles. In his sleep the old man breathed with a soft sound between a snore and a moan.

The old man. He didn't seem Indian.

But Calvin had made that mistake once before. He had been half asleep then too—it seemed long ago now—watching his fish line slant into the drifting green Snake Creek, when he heard hooves clattering on the gravel. Four Indians —two braves, a squaw, and a boy—splashed into the shallows downstream from him. They were so close Calvin could see the eagle feather dangling from the rope tied cruelly around the lead pony's jaw as a bit. Calvin dug his fingernails into his palms to keep from moving, and they didn't look his way.

The lead brave jerked up his pony to let the others cross ahead of him. The mustang danced sideways along the gravel bar, rolling his eyes. A half-grown, mangy puppy trailed out of the brush after them. The mustang kicked sideways, wrapping the dog around his heel and sailing him, bent like a broken bow, into the bulrushes.

The Indian slammed the butt of his rifle between the pony's ears and then hauled back on the rope, twisting the plunging pony's head around until he was standing still, trembling. The Indian slid down and, holding the rope with one hand, picked up the dog by the scruff of the neck, swung back up onto the pony and kicked him into a gallop across the shallow creek.

Calvin ran all the way home. He found his father in the barn shelling corn for chicken feed. As Calvin told him about the Indians his father kept rubbing off the hard kernels with the heels of his hands. When Calvin said, "But he didn't leave him there," his father looked up, smiling. "I mean he picked him up and carried him," Calvin explained. He reached out and scratched Shep's back, making him thump his hind foot in ecstasy. "Just like a white man would. He didn't even seem Indian when he did that."

His father laughed. "He was just thinking about dinner."

"Do you mean . . ."

His father nodded, going back to the corn. "Sure. Nothing an Indian likes better than roast dog."

Calvin jerked and sat up. What was he doing here with an Indian? He looked around and then up through the hole the dying fire bored into the night, and that made him think of the well.

Maybe the buffalo hunters were around here after all. Maybe they had caught up with the herd and then camped to skin their kill. They might have camped several days to smoke some meat. They might even come back to the river for water, or to leave a cache of hides to pick up on their way back east.

Calvin poked through the fire until he found a charred branch. Watching the Indian over his shoulder, he crawled away. When he was deep in the trees he stood up and felt his way to a big smooth trunk. The papery bark peeled away in his hands. A sycamore. He peered at it in the dark, searching for a flat place. On the river side he chopped out two big slashes, one as high as he could reach, and the other level with his knees. Between them he lettered with the charred stick:

HELP   HELP
LOST BOY

He paused. Should he write, "Indian prisoner"? That didn't seem right, and besides, tomorrow he would have the raft. One way or another, he would be on the river.

He wrote, "HEADED SOUTH," and then, on the way back to the campfire he blazed some other trees nearby to make the message sing out. It would wash off in the first rain, but it was something.

SIX

The Talking Leaves

"I DON'T UNDERSTAND you," Calvin said. The Indian had stopped on the spine of a little hill to look back at the smoke of their fire, a gray flower blooming white at the top and bending toward the sun in the morning breeze. "You didn't put the fire out. You just made it smoke."

"My son and the Worm will go back to the cave for me," the Indian said. "I left a letter for them there. I told them I would make smoke along the way so they could follow me."

"Who? Did you say 'worm'?"

The Indian didn't answer. He shifted the blanket roll that was draped across one shoulder and tied under his other arm.

"What do you mean, a letter?" Calvin said.

The Indian started walking again, without answering.

Calvin followed, already limping a little as yesterday's blister woke up. "I don't understand you. Are you trying to bring the Comanche?"

No answer.

What was this talk about "the worm"? Some Indian hocus pocus about death? Was "going home" and "the worm" the way Indians talk about getting ready to die? And what kind of a letter did he mean? He spoke English. Maybe he could read and write too. Impossible. A lot of Indians spoke a few words of English—understood more than they let on usually. This one happened to know quite a lot, that was all. Reading and writing means school. Civilization. Not hiding in caves and killing white women. Whatever the Indian was marking in that stolen ledger was just some sort of Indian signs. A charm, maybe, for the spirit of a long-dead son and "the worm" of death to find.

Miles later, when yesterday's sunburn was heating up, Calvin could still see the smudge of smoke against the hot blue sky behind them. The Indian limped along just as fast today. Calvin wondered if he had a blister too. His greased moccasins looked softer than Calvin's rain-stiff boots.

He studied the Indian's limp. It seemed to be stiff-kneed, rather than footsore. The next time Calvin caught up with him the Indian had his head back and seemed to be sniffing the breeze. Calvin sat down, took off his left boot to look at the old blister, and asked, "Are you trying to catch up with your tribe?"

The Indian shook his head. "My people lived in the mountains," he said.

"Mountains?" Calvin said. "What mountains?"

"We called the place *Echota*," the Indian said. "It's on a river the whites call the Tennessee."

"Tennessee? Why, that's hundreds of miles from here."

The Indian nodded. "Your foot hurts from this little trail," he said. "You should have made the trip from Echota."

"What trip?" Calvin said, stamping his foot back into the rain-stiff boot.

The Indian gestured over his shoulder. "Out to the Arkansas country. North of here, but far from Echota. It took us seventy days and seventy nights. We went in flat-boats—a hundred and eight warriors, and two hundred women and children. We pulled the boats up the narrow parts, and hunters followed along the banks to bring meat for the evening. In the deep water the boats drifted with the current, and I taught the young men . . ."

He paused and stood looking out across the patchy grass and mesquite bushes, eyes narrowed as if he were watching something far away. Finally Calvin said, "You taught the young men?"

The Indian nodded. "When we got to the Arkansas country, all the young men could read." He started walking again. Calvin pushed the butt of the rifle into the ground to shove himself back onto his feet and hurried to catch up.

"Read?" Calvin said. "Can you read?"

"Yes, I can read. The Cherokee can read—I gave them that. But some of them say I took their mountains. And Echota. Some of them say I made them lose Echota. And their big river with the corn and beans and pumpkins growing in the lowlands."

Calvin shook his head. "What do you mean? How could you take a river?"

"Did you say your father was a judge?"

"That's right."

"He tells people what to do?"

"Not exactly. He tells them what the law says they have to do."

The Indian nodded. "Someone has to decide what the people must do. Some of us decided that the people had to leave Echota. It wasn't what we wanted, any of us. But we signed the treaties because we decided the whites would make us leave anyway. And they did. Even those who said we didn't speak for them had to leave too. With soldiers behind them. They lost their mountains, but I gave them the talking leaves."

"Talking leaves?"

"Paper that talks. Writing."

"I don't understand," Calvin said. "Do you mean the Cherokee can read? Read English words?"

The Indian shook his head. He paused and looked around, wrinkling his pinched nose.

"I smell death," he said.

Calvin swung the rifle up level at his hip. "Death? What death?"

The Indian looked down at him—he was only a little taller than Calvin, but he always seemed to look down—and smiled, downwardly also. "My own, perhaps. But not just yet."

He walked on, head bobbing with his limp, but still covering more ground with his step and a half than Calvin covered with two. Calvin levered the breech half open to be sure there was a shell under the hammer and then followed.

A breeze stirred the grass, and then Calvin smelled it too—something was dead nearby.

The Indian was moving more carefully now, keeping in the trees and running stooped over across the open places. Calvin followed, stooping and running in the same places.

A shadow crossed his face. Calvin ducked, and looked up. A turkey buzzard sailed just above the tops of the trees, skinny neck stretched out straight and warty red head turned sideways to watch the ground with one eye.

A little farther Calvin came to the Indian, sitting on his heels in a thicket of persimmons. As far as Calvin could see, the prairie was mounded with black humps, like a giant gopher city. The stink of death was thick as fog. Two buzzards flapped heavily away from one of the mounds, and then Calvin realized that they were dead animals. Had another wagon train been slaughtered by Indians here?

"Who did that?" he asked.

"Buffalo hunters," the Indian said. "These they skinned. Sometimes they kill hundreds of buffalo and only take the tongues."

Buffalo hunters. Calvin stood up and squinted, looking across the prairie for the two hunters with the white pack mule—looking for the way home. All he saw were carcasses, buzzards and yellow grasshoppers.

"How would you like just a little of that meat they left to rot in the sun?" the Indian said.

"Some of it might be all right," Calvin said.

The Indian twisted the corners of his mouth down and shook his head. "All it's good for now is buzzards and beetles and green flies," he said. He stood up and went on.

A little farther they came to a place where wagons had crossed. The river was high now, but even after the storm the tracks were plain in the prairie. The Indian stopped and studied them.

"These must be the tracks of our wagons," Calvin said. He looked up at the sun and then squinted at the two lines of bent grass. "They're headed east and north—they're ours."

The Indian nodded. "The buffalo hunters crossed here too, going the other way," he said, pointing to hoof marks stamped over the wheel ruts. "Up ahead there the river turns away from the direction I want to go, and it seems to get wider. We'll build a raft and cross here."

They walked along the bank until the Indian stopped at a brush pile against a big double-trunked hickory in the slack overflow. He waded out, broke off a dead limb and used it as a lever to pry logs loose from the tangle of driftwood. A water snake fell off one of the dead branches and traced an S through the brown water almost under the Indian's arm. He stepped back and poked at it with the tree branch, spitting out a strange word. The snake dived.

The Indian looked over at Calvin, who was standing on the bank watching, and said, "Listen to yourself say that thing."

"Do you mean *snake*?"

The Indian nodded. "*Snake*—do you hear it? It's a good word. It sounds like what it means. Some of our words do too. When I first started to make the talking leaves I tried to do them that way—with pictures of animals that sound like the words. But there were too many." He turned back to the brush pile. "Here, help me. This one is our raft."

It was just a small forked log with the two arms longer than the tail. It had been dead so long that the bark was gone, and as they hauled it out of the pile, Calvin noticed that it floated high in the water, as if it had baked out dry and light in the sun a long time before the river flooded high enough to reach it.

They dragged it as far out of the water as they could and then, with Calvin helping, the Indian cut and trimmed saplings to deck over the space between the arms. As he fitted them into place he notched both arms so that the saplings nested solidly. Half a dozen saplings made an uneven deck twice as wide as a wagon seat. When the Indian went into the woods Calvin stayed behind, studying the raft. It looked as if it would float all the way to civilization. He looked down the river. It was already shrinking toward its old banks, leaving high-water anklets of broken twigs and leaves at the feet of the trees.

The Indian came back trailing two long skinned poles. He laid them across the raft and then put his blanket roll beside them. Calvin laid the rifle along the other side. They waded out knee-deep, and then, while the Indian held the raft, Calvin climbed aboard. The Indian heaved himself up, the slow current took the raft and they began to drift.

The Indian showed Calvin how to use the pole to angle the raft along, tail first, through the current. Once, when Calvin tried to push too hard, the pole stuck in the muddy bottom and almost pulled him off. After that, he just nudged the raft out with little shoves, keeping the pole close to the side. The river had overflowed both banks, so that Calvin estimated it was a quarter of a mile wide there. When they got over the normal channel, their poles couldn't reach the bottom. The Indian probed for the bottom occasionally as the shoreline slid slowly past.

He made a gesture with one hand, somehow making a little motion mean everything around them. "This is the way it was many days on the way to the Arkansas country."

"What did you mean when you said you taught young men to read on that trip?" Calvin asked. "Do you mean really read English words?"

The Indian shook his head. "Cherokee words." He smiled at the expression on Calvin's face.

"Did you ever have an idea catch hold of you so that you couldn't get away from it?" the Indian asked.

Calvin shook his head. "I guess I don't understand."

"Well, did you ever see a squirrel fall from the top of a tree and land on the ground without hurting himself? Did you ever see one do that, and wonder how?"

"No," Calvin said. "I never saw that."

"Didn't you ever see something *like* that? Something you can't understand? Something you wondered about?"

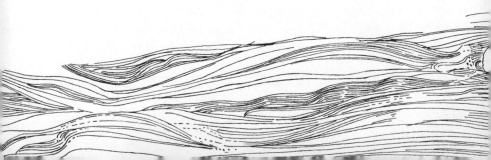

Calvin thought for a moment. "I have wondered about spiders."

"Spiders?"

Calvin nodded, turning his eyes away. "I always wondered how they get their web across a high place. I mean, how do they get the first strand across? From then on I can understand. They just walk out on the first one and let themselves down, spinning as they go. But I wonder how they get the first one across?"

The Indian smiled. "I don't know. It must be simple. If you could just see the web in the right way, the answer must be there, don't you think? Right there."

Calvin nodded.

The Indian picked up the pole and ran it deep into the brown water, feeling for bottom. The pull of the current turned him half around, and the pole twisted in his hand as the other end bobbed up behind them. He laid it dripping across the Y nose of the raft.

"Starting to write was the same way," he went on. "It seemed so easy. Just a mark for each word, or something simple like that. At first I thought I could probably do it in a day or two. I cut some smooth hickory chips and started marking a different sign for each word. But there were too many words. Then I decided to make one mark for each sound. It seemed so simple, if I could just hear the sounds right. I thought I had it then—just a day or two, again.

"Then I thought perhaps in a moon. . . . How old are you, boy?"

"Fifteen," Calvin said.

"It took almost that long. It took twelve years and a

mountain of hickory chips with shapes carved on them and then thrown away."

"Twelve years?" Calvin said. "You worked on it twelve years?"

The Indian nodded. "My children grew up hearing me sound words over and over. The people in the village heard me talking to myself. They went behind my house and saw the stacks of hickory chips with the strange marks. They said I was a witch. Even my wife was afraid. At first she helped me, but then she began to complain that I was letting weeds grow in the corn. One day she burned down the cabin, with all my hickory chips. She said she was afraid of the magic I was making." He smiled a little. "But I think she wanted me to help her in the fields too."

"I don't understand you," Calvin said. "Were you trying to invent a written language all by yourself?"

The Indian shook his head. "The language was there. I just had to hear it. Nobody had ever heard it right before. My little girl heard it better than anyone. She heard the sounds that made it simple."

A twist of the current shoved their raft toward the far bank. The Indian picked up his pole and slid it into the water ahead of them so that the raft drifted past it. When the pole was straight up and down it touched bottom, and he gave the raft a slight sideways nudge toward the bank.

Calvin sat on the other edge to keep the raft from tipping.

"You're wondering why I'm telling you these things now."

Calvin nodded.

The Indian ran his pole into the water ahead again. This

time the top of the pole came out of the water a few inches as they drifted by, and he gave the raft a good shove. "Because when we get to the other bank I'm going to start across the prairie. I want you to go with me."

Calvin reached for the rifle. "No. I'm going to take the raft on down the river."

"What do you know about traveling a river? This is a long, slow, twisting river. You don't know where it will take you."

"Eventually, it will take me to a ranch, or a town. I'll find some way to get home from there."

The Indian shrugged. "Or it may take you to a Comanche village. I want you to stay with me. I've been trying to make you understand that I'm not a wild Indian, like the Comanche, so you will stay with me."

"Why?" Calvin asked. "You're not really afraid of—I mean, about the ears strung on a stick. You're not really afraid of white people, are you?"

The Indian nodded. "Yes, I'm afraid of whites."

"Well, then, don't you know that taking a white prisoner could make it bad for you?"

The Indian didn't answer for a moment. "I hadn't thought of that. I hadn't thought that taking care of a lost boy, and feeding him . . . I suppose it would depend on what you said."

Calvin looked away. The Indian went on. "But I do have another reason."

"What is it?"

"My daughter brought talking leaves back from the

Arkansas country—letters that told the people in Echota what we found out here."

"Out here?"

"Out here away from Echota. In the Arkansas country. They told about the river and the hills and the corn we planted and the town we built called *Tahlequah*. And perhaps, if my son and the Worm do not find us before we get to Mexico, you will have to take a letter back to Tahlequah for me."

"I don't want to go there. Or Mexico either. Why are you going to Mexico, anyway?"

"That's what you may have to explain to the people."

"I may have to explain! Look, I don't want to be some kind of a messenger for you. I understand that you're different from the Comanche, all right. But you're Indian, and I'm white. You want to go someplace. I don't understand what it's all about, but it doesn't have anything to do with me. I just want to go home."

The Indian didn't answer. Instead, he reached inside his shirt and brought out a disk, half the size of a saucer, that was strung on the chain around his neck. He slipped the chain over his head, ducking a little to work it over his turban. The disk twisted back and forth, flashing in the sun, and Calvin could see it was silver. The Indian handed it to Calvin, picked up his pole again and began working them in to the bank.

"What's this?" Calvin asked. He remembered that yesterday he had decided the chain probably held the locket of a murdered white woman.

"Something to show you that what I say is true. So you'll believe you're safer with me than alone on the river."

It looked like a big coin. On one side was molded the head of a man with two long Indian pipes crossed above it. There were some strange marks above the pipes, and alongside the marks was engraved "Presented to George Gist by the General Council of the Cherokee Nation, for his ingenuity in the invention of the Cherokee alphabet, 1825."

The molded head wore a turban. "Is this you?" Calvin asked. The Indian was pushing hard now against the current that ran faster in the shallow water. "Is your name George Gist?" Calvin asked.

"My Cherokee name is Sequoyah. My white name is George Gist."

"Why do you have two names?"

"Because I lived on the edge of the two worlds. White and Indian. I had a name for each."

"And you really did invent an alphabet," Calvin said, trying the words out loud to see if he could believe it.

"That was the easy part," the Indian said. "Some of the letters I took from an English language newspaper. Others I just made up. The hard part was hearing the sounds in the right way to give meaning to the marks." He held his hand out and Calvin put the medal back in it.

"Which way are you going?" Calvin asked.

The Indian pointed across the prairie. "Buffalo crossed here," he said. "They are traveling south. So am I. If we can catch up with them we will have meat again. If I can have honey when I'm sick and meat when I'm well, I will get there. But we will have to trail carefully. Comanche follow the buffalo." He stood up and jumped from the raft onto the drowned grass at the water's edge. "And so do the white hunters."

Calvin hesitated. The raft rocked against the bank and he moved toward the center to steady it. The Indian climbed the shallow bank, walked out into the grass, and then unrolled his blanket and took out the brass kettle and the leather-bound journal. He came back to the river and scooped a little water into the kettle. Then he walked downstream into the trees. Calvin sat on the raft.

He wasn't going to Mexico, that was for sure. But now floating down the river until he came to a white settlement didn't seem so easy. He looked around. Out on the prairie at least he could see all the way to the sky in every direction. Here he couldn't see past the screen of leaves along the bank. When he moved, the rustles and scampers stopped, and Calvin could feel eyes on him.

The river would eventually get to a white settlement, but where would it get to first?

The Indian came back carrying four black walnuts, stripping off the fleshy green outer hulls with his knife as he walked. He squatted on his heels next to the kettle and scraped the pulpy black fibers from inside the walnut hulls into the water. He set the kettle aside, walked to the bank again and cut a thin whip of a branch.

"What are you doing?" Calvin asked.

"Making magic," the Indian said, whittling the stick to a point. He went back to the kettle and stirred the walnut scrapings with the sharpened stick. He tore a page from the journal, dipped the stick into the walnut dye and marked on it.

"You're writing a message, aren't you?" Calvin said.

The Indian looked up and smiled, turning the corners of his thin mouth down as if to deny the smile as he made it.

"I'm saying words in my head and putting marks on this paper. Sometime, my son and the Worm may look at these marks and hear my words. Isn't that magic?"

Calvin scrambled off the raft, climbed the bank and looked over the Indian's shoulder. He recognized a shape like an R, another like a D and another like a G. Others looked like no letters he had ever seen.

"Does it look hard?" the Indian asked.

Calvin grinned and nodded. "My father says that Indian talk sounds like somebody wading and chopping wood at the same time. That looks like trying to spell it."

"How long did it take you to learn to read and write your way?" the Indian asked.

"I don't know—three years, I guess. Maybe four."

"A Cherokee boy can learn to read and write in three days." He pointed to a character like an R. "I took some of the white man's letters and gave them Cherokee sounds. Now the Cherokee can read and write their own language."

He folded the paper, lettering inside, and wedged it into the willow fork. "I'll leave a letter for my son and the Worm, who will follow us if they can."

"Where are they?"

"They went ahead to find horses. After the Tewockenees stole ours."

"Ahead? They're up ahead somewhere?"

"Perhaps. But if they find horses they will go back to the cave where they left me."

"Why did they leave you?"

"I was too sick to keep going on foot. They left me in the cave until they could find horses for us."

"Why didn't you stay there, then?"

"The cave is full of river, don't you remember?"

"Sure, but you could have camped around there somewhere and waited."

"I am an old man, and sick. I may not have time to wait. I left a letter for them there saying that I am going on to Mexico, and that I would light fires along the way so they can follow me. Here I will leave another letter. If they can, they will follow me. If not, you and I must do it alone."

Calvin shook his head and took a step back, as the Indian walked to the edge of the bank and jammed the sharpened butt of the tree into the soft mud so that it stood up like a little flagpole with the paper at the top.

"When we went from Echota to the Arkansas country, we traveled a much bigger river than this one. We had boats too, not just a raft made of driftwood. But there were many places when the river turned into rocks and we had to carry the boats. There were storms. There were long times when there was no meat, even though we had many hunters."

Calvin didn't say anything. Beyond the Indian's shoulder he could see where horses had climbed the muddy bank. Horses wearing iron shoes. There were white men up ahead, the way the Indian was going.

Calvin looked away from the Indian into the mottled

water. He tried to bring up his father's face, but the sunlight made yellow grasshopper faces instead, and so he looked back at the old man. The Indian, he reminded himself.

"Have—have you ever eaten dog?"

The Indian tilted his head to one side. "No," he said. "Is it good?"

Calvin laughed. "I'll go with you a ways," he said, looking past the Indian at the tracks of the buffalo hunters leading across the prairie.

SEVEN

Hoofbeats

THE NEXT morning the Indian boiled two kettles of water. The first they drank with the end of the meat and honey, the other the Indian soaked up in scraps of the deer hide. "This will give us something wet to chew until we find more water," he said, packing the soaked scraps back into the kettle.

They left the cover of the trees, with the smoke from the Indian's signal fire rising behind them, following the highway grazed across the prairie.

Buzzards were scattered overhead as thick as the buffalo chips scattered along the ground, and twice that day they passed a big arch of stained bones feathered with feasting birds. The buzzards stared at Calvin and the Indian, hopped heavily away, flapping but not flying, and then waddled back to the carcass as soon as they had passed.

As they topped a small rise, the Indian dropped to his

knees and pointed across the prairie. Calvin saw an antelope picking his stick-legged way down the slope ahead of them. The antelope stopped and looked back, legs cocked for a leap.

The Indian slapped his own shoulder lightly. "Steady the barrel on me," he said. "And aim low. It's easy to overshoot downhill."

Calvin laid the barrel across the Indian's shoulder, took a deep breath and drew the sights together. The antelope danced two nervous steps and paused again, held a moment by curiosity. Calvin swung the sights after him, trying to hurry.

Just before he fired, the Indian said something.

The shot rolled across the prairie like thunder, but the antelope floated away, legs tucked up and tail flirting at the top of his leap as if daring Calvin to try again. By the time he levered another shell into the chamber the antelope looked like a jackrabbit bounding across the grazed-over buffalo grass.

Suddenly Calvin was hungrier than ever.

"You threw me off," he said. The Indian sank down off his knees and sat in the grass, mopping his forehead with his sleeve. He didn't answer.

"What was it you said, just before I fired?" Calvin asked.

"It was Cherokee."

"Cherokee? Why would you talk to me in Cherokee?"

"I was talking to the antelope. I was asking the pardon."

"Asking the pardon? What do you mean?"

"It is the Cherokee way. To us the deer, the woods, and the streams and the Cherokee are all part of the same thing.

When we kill a part, we ask a pardon. The white deer is the spirit of all the deer and so we ask his pardon. I suppose there is a white antelope too."

Calvin dropped the butt of the rifle so hard the breech rattled. "White antelope!" he said.

The Indian looked up at him, sweat glistening in the Bible-cover wrinkles of his face.

"Next time," Calvin said, "say your charms without jiggling the rifle."

The Indian's voice was as expressionless as his face. "Did I move the rifle, or did you overshoot?"

Calvin hesitated.

The Indian slipped the blanket roll off his shoulder and rummaged through it until he came up with half a box of rifle shells. He held his hand out for the rifle, and without thinking, Calvin handed it to him. The Indian slipped a new round into the magazine and handed it back.

"Where two worlds meet they make a lonely place," he said.

Calvin looked around at the prairie stretching away forever on every side. "What do you mean?"

"I mean there's a boy's world and a man's world. In a boy's world it's always someone else's fault."

He stood up, shouldered the blanket roll again and started down the slope. Calvin fell into step alongside him this time, instead of following. After a while he said, "What if you forgot to ask the pardon of the white deer?"

"The Cherokee believe that the hunter will get sick. Rheumatism, probably, or something else."

"The Cherokee believe," Calvin said. "Do you believe?"

"About the rheumatism?"

Calvin nodded.

The Indian rubbed his elbow. "Who knows what puts the pain in a man's joints?"

"Is rheumatism what makes you limp?"

The Indian shook his head. "My limp doesn't come from the white deer. It comes from the white general. Andy Jackson. Have you heard of him?"

"Andrew Jackson was President," Calvin said. "The President of the United States."

"When I knew him he was a general. Fighting the Creeks and the French, in the mountains where the Cherokee lived."

"Did he shoot you in the leg?"

"No, we were fighting on his side. He called us Morgan's Cherokee Regiment. We always fought the Creeks, and since Jackson was fighting them, we fought with Jackson. I got a sore leg out of that, and Jackson got to be President. Then he took away our lands."

"President Jackson did?"

"His government. It was sign the papers or have the soldiers come. I knew about soldiers. There were too many. Too many soldiers and too many guns. And we had already had the measles and the smallpox. I knew there were too many, and so I signed. For that some of the people call me coward, and traitor. But they don't know what it would have been like."

"Are you a chief, then?"

"No. This was something for the councils to decide, but they could not agree. It had to be decided. Many people looked to me because I had taught them the talking leaves and because I had been to the Arkansas country and knew what was out here in the West. When I signed, many people decided to come."

He stooped and slipped the blanket roll back over his shoulder. When they started again it seemed to Calvin that the Indian limped more than before. After a while he noticed that the Indian had slipped the medal out of his shirt and was rubbing his fingers across it as he walked.

"Some tried to stay, but then the soldiers came and marched them out," he said, as if he had been carrying on the same conversation in his mind all this time. "Maybe I was wrong. Maybe if we had all stayed, and hidden in the hills and fought . . . But we couldn't agree, and someone had to decide."

They walked on. After a long time Calvin looked back. The trees along the river were out of sight now, and the sun seemed to sit on the back of his head. "We'll dry up out here today," he said.

The Indian stopped, unpacked the brass kettle and handed Calvin one of the wet strips of hide. Before he put one in his own mouth he said, "This is the way to Mexico." Then he shouldered the blanket roll again and limped away.

Calvin looked back in the direction of the raft and the river. Was he really any safer with this Indian? Out here where even the bunch grass dried up and died, and where the Indian's smoke signal might bring the Comanche? And besides, the Indian was going the wrong way.

"Come."

The voice was so close that Calvin started. The Indian had walked silently back and stood now, eyes narrowed against the sun, looking into Calvin as he had the first day, back in the cave.

Calvin shook his head. "Why?" he said, trying to break his eyes away. "Tell me why you're going to Mexico. What is it you have to do down there? What do you want me to help you do?"

"I can't explain it to you now. I could say most of it in Cherokee but only part of it in your words, and this is not the time to try. If you can believe me . . . Everyone has to decide what he can believe. Stay with me if you can."

He turned away again, and this time Calvin was sure he wouldn't look back. The turban caught the sunlight and Calvin thought again of the pictures of Moses and Abraham in the Bible at home. He looked back once more and then he shouldered his blanket roll and followed.

Twice that afternoon they jumped over rain-carved gullies that held water, but the buffalo had been there ahead of them, wallowing in the water until it was a stinking muck. Once they came to a discouraged outpost of stunted cedars. The Indian dug around the roots with the tomahawk but found no water.

Later the Indian stopped again and knelt, head close to the ground. Calvin could see no sign of water there, and the Indian stood up after a moment and went on without digging. Later he stopped again and put his ear to the ground.

Calvin stood over him, dust-caked inside and out and thinking about the river that was so far away now. "I suppose you think you can hear water," he said.

The Indian looked up and smiled in his downward way. "I hear horses," he said.

Calvin dropped to his knees and listened. "I can't hear anything," he said.

"Wait a while. It starts and stops. Our tracks are hard to find in this buffalo trail, and so they are coming very carefully."

Calvin pressed his ear back to the ground, but all he could hear was the rising pulse of his own heart. Finally, he felt, rather than heard, a rumble. He sat up and nodded.

"How many?" he asked.

The Indian shook his head. "Not many. One, maybe two."

"How far?"

The Indian shrugged. "Close enough. Coming closer. But I don't understand why he's coming so slowly."

The Indian slipped his skinning knife out of his belt and began cutting bunches of the buffalo grass. "Find a gully or a hollow. Over there." Calvin started across the trampled ground, and he could hear the Indian running unevenly behind him.

A line of wind-scoured rock poked a few inches out of the prairie like the edge of some huge buried shell. Calvin threw himself down behind it, trying to squirm flat as a shadow. The Indian dropped beside him and then propped himself up on one elbow to sprinkle the cut buffalo grass over their legs.

Calvin put his ear to the rock. He could hear the hoof-beats clearer now. They seemed to come in a little rush, stop, and then come on again.

"Keep your head down until I tell you," the Indian said. "Maybe this is Tessee and the Worm. Or maybe it is someone else. He is trailing strangely. Take your hat off and lie on it—and keep your head down behind the rock."

Tiny brown ants scrambled along the edge of the rock. With his face in the dirt Calvin could see their world, a place of grass trunks, seed boulders and a huge dead beetle—all invisible above the grass. The ants made him think of the yellow grasshopper as the hoofbeats pounded in his ear.

He pressed against the ground, holding his breath. One of the ants half stood up on its rear legs and waved its antennae. The hoofs were louder now, right on top of them.

"Keep your head down," the Indian whispered. Calvin heard the tiny rustle of the Indian's shirt as he raised himself to look over the rock. A thought flashed by: hoofbeats didn't have to be Comanche—they could be the buffalo hunters.

He heard the Indian laugh quietly through his nose. Calvin realized he had been holding his own breath, and he let it out with a sigh that blew the ant over backward. The Indian reached for the rifle between them, but Calvin held on to it. The hoofbeats were going away now.

"Who is it?" Calvin whispered.

"Let me have the rifle—hurry," the Indian said.

Calvin raised his head above the rock. There was Shep! Just the way he used to wait by the creek, ears up, tongue lolling out the side of his jaws, and head cocked, ready to come wagging all over at Calvin's whistle. Another dog shape drifted into view, and then Calvin recognized them: prairie wolves!

A third wolf bellied along the ground toward a large, shapeless black mass beyond them. The mass moved, and Calvin saw it was a shaggy buffalo. When the buffalo shook his horns, the wolf jumped back and stopped, half-turned and ready to run.

"Let me have the rifle," the Indian said, out loud this time.

At the sound the wolf in front of them jumped up, spinning around to face them with teeth bared and looking nothing like Shep now, and then he loped off down the slope toward the buffalo. The bull heaved back onto his feet, scattering the wolves. Calvin let the Indian take the rifle.

The buffalo scrambled a few steps and then fell to his knees again. Calvin recognized the sound, the flurry of hoofbeats and then a pause, that he had heard with his ear to the ground. One of the wolves closed in and the bull stood up again, shaking his horns.

The Indian sat hunched forward, elbows on knees, sighting carefully. Calvin heard the shot and then the separate *thunk* of the slug slamming into the buffalo, knocking him over the way Calvin's breath had swept the ant over. The wolves disappeared, as if into the ground.

Calvin stood up, but the Indian sat still, elbows on knees, watching the buffalo.

"Come on. You got him," Calvin said.

Just then the buffalo kicked. He struggled onto his belly, pawing dust, got his feet under him and lurched up. He took three tottering steps before the Indian shot again. This time he collapsed as if a rope had been jerked across his hocks. The Indian levered out the empty shell and waited.

"That finished him," Calvin said.

"He's an old bull," the Indian said. "Probably sick. He's come a long way by himself, with wolves behind him. He won't stop except to die."

The bull took longer to find his feet this time. The third shot staggered him but he stayed up, turning the stagger into a broken trot that carried him over a little rise and out of sight.

The Indian stood and walked with Calvin to the edge of the rise. Blood puddled black in the dust there, already drawing green flies. They could see the buffalo run and fall, and then run again, shrinking into the endless prairie. Three smoke shapes drifted along behind him, stopping now and then to sniff at the fresh blood.

They followed, out of the grazed-over buffalo grass into higher ground, where raw gullies cut through low hills and stunted bushes speckled the dust with shade. Calvin's tongue felt rough as a cat's, and his throat was so dry and swollen it hurt to speak.

"How long can he keep going?"

The Indian mopped his forehead with the loose sleeve of his shirt. "When a sheep is down he is dead. Even if the wolf leaves him, a sheep will lie there and die. But a bull will stand up and go on."

"Why? Is he trying to catch up with the herd?"

The Indian shook his head. "I don't think so. I think it is something he must do because he is a bull. Some animals are like that."

Calvin stopped. "And some men?"

"Yes, some men too."

"Like you?"

The Indian went on without answering.

"That's it, isn't it?" Calvin called after him. "You don't really have any reason to go to Mexico, do you? Did someone say you couldn't do it, like they said you couldn't do the talking leaves?"

Now the Indian stopped and looked back. He twisted a slight downward smile. "The Worm said that, yes. When they left me to look for horses."

"And now you have to prove you can."

He nodded. "There's that. There's always that with me. I've always lived on the edge of two worlds, and so I suppose I'm always proving something. But that's not the only . . . There's more than that for going to Mexico."

Calvin sat down in a tiny puddle of shade beside a boulder. "Not for me, there's not. I'm tired. You go on if you want to be a bull. I'm tired and thirsty and I don't want to go to Mexico anyway."

The Indian's voice was a hoarse rustle. "You don't want! What do you think I want? Just to prove I can make a hard trail? I've gone back and forth from Echota to Arkansas

twice. I've fought a war. I've made talking leaves and
taught a whole nation how to read and write them. Now
I'm thinkng about an arithmetic. A Cherokee way of counting in big numbers. I'm lame and sick and tired and I've
seen seventy summers. Do you think I want to spend my
last one on this prairie?"

He went on. Calvin watched him stumble into a small
gully, pull himself up again without looking back, and climb
out of sight over the ridge.

Calvin thought of the buffalo and then of the way he had
tried to explain in his mind to his father—how long ago?—
why he was following this Indian. Out loud, he said, "He's
not just milling around, that's for sure. He's going somewhere." And then, "Maybe I shouldn't have followed him
in the first place, but I wasn't doing so well by myself. Now
I've come this far . . ."

When he stood up the sun hit so hard that he leaned
against the boulder a moment before he started again,
scrambling over the shaley slope to catch up.

EIGHT

Smoke

BEFORE THEY came to the dead buffalo they heard the wolves fighting. Following the sound, they climbed along outcropping rock ribs over a little hill.

The bull had fallen stretched out, lurching forward a last time. One of the wolves, probably a female, Calvin thought, was worrying open a gash on the shaggy neck. The other two were circling each other and snarling, neck ruffs up and teeth bared. The Indian flipped a rock at them and they were gone.

"They were fighting over more than they could eat in a week," he said. "When we butcher this bull there will be some blood. Watch out for them when they smell it."

They didn't try to skin the buffalo. As the wolves watched from a low ridge, and Calvin watched the wolves, the Indian peeled back the tough hide from the rump and loins and then hacked out big chunks of dark meat. He sliced two thin strips and handed one to Calvin.

"Just chew it," he said. "Spit it out when it goes dry." Calvin hesitated.

"We may be a long way from water," the Indian said as he put the other strip in his own mouth.

Calvin looked at the bloody strip, his stomach rising at the slimy touch on his fingers. The Indian propped up the heavy head and cut out the tongue.

"Tonight we'll cook some of this," he said. "We'll sear it first on a hot fire so the juice stays in it. The juice that kept him going. When we eat him, we'll have it in us."

"Is that magic?"

The Indian paused. "Maybe so. Like makes like—that's the idea of magic."

"But do you really believe that?"

"I don't know. It is something to think about when I feel sick and want to quit." He was wrapping the slabs of bloody meat in the deerskin, handing Calvin some to carry. "When that happens, it helps to remember how long the buffalo kept going and know that you have the juice of him. And besides, there's no water."

Without looking at it, Calvin put the meat in his mouth and chewed down some of the raw juice. The Indian jabbed the knife in the ground several times to clean it, slipped the blanket roll over his shoulder and started again, face to the afternoon sun. Calvin struggled into his own blanket roll and followed.

He looked back once. Two of the wolves were feeding.

Calvin thought of the bloody meat he was carrying and wondered if perhaps the third might be following them. He glanced around, but he saw only prairie.

Sun.

Dust.

Thirst.

Yellow grasshoppers.

He tried thinking about the buffalo, but he couldn't fix his mind on anything except how hot and tired and thirsty he was. Something cool . . . the springhouse, back home. A limestone cave in the bluff behind the house, spongy with moss underfoot, a black pool with crocks of sweet cream, wooden tubs of butter and sometimes a striped melon floating in it, water spilling over a glass-smooth lip of rock, tooth-aching cold. . . . Water.

He looked around and the Indian was gone. Calvin stopped. He was alone. The edges of the prairie rushed away from him again into the hard blue sky, and there was the same bug face staring solemnly at him from a swaying ragweed stalk. A choked cry squeezed out of his dry throat before he turned around and saw the Indian several steps behind him, shading his face with his hand.

Calvin coughed to mask the cry, and then, forcing his voice to its lowest range, he said, "What are you doing?"

"I thought I heard a turtle dove," the Indian said. Calvin listened. Gnats whined around his ears. The Indian pointed, and Calvin saw the slate-gray bird fly across the setting sun. The Indian started in that direction, saying, "Doves fly into the prairie, but at night they roost in dead trees. And before they roost they drink."

Calvin followed, thinking that if they came to another stinking buffalo wallow he might not be able to keep from drinking. But as the sun went from yellow to orange to red to purple they climbed into steeper hills, and Calvin remembered they had left the buffalo trail back on the prairie.

It was almost dusk when he saw the smoke.

He dropped to his knees and the Indian squatted, sitting on his heels. This was not the whisper of a cautious hunter's fire, but a thick pall, hanging low in the evening calm beyond the ridge of a hill ahead of them.

"Whose fire do you think that is?" Calvin asked.

The Indian looked around at him and smiled downwardly. "Indians and whites, their fires smoke the same."

"But what do you think?"

The Indian shrugged. "It's a lot of smoke. Buffalo hunters curing some meat, maybe. Or a large band of Comanche. Tessee and the Worm, maybe, answering my smoke fires. A rancher, maybe. That much smoke could be coming from a chimney. But whoever built that big fire probably camped near water. I'm waiting for darkness. Then we will see."

Calvin sagged down to one hip, knees still doubled under him. After a while he straightened his legs.

Sequoyah squatted on his heels, eyes fixed far off on the drifting smoke, without moving.

An owl whistled, and the sound seemed to come from everywhere at once. A bobcat screamed, like a baby crying, and Calvin shivered.

To make himself sit still he played a silent game. He thought about each itch, tickle and sore spot, one at a time. Then he decided which was the most uncomfortable. The first time it was his left foot, which was going to sleep. Now he started counting inside his head, promising himself a move when he got to a hundred. At seventy-five his foot was all needles and sparks and he began to hurry, but he touched every number to a hundred before he moved. Then he began to think about his uncomfortable spots one at a time again to select a new worst one.

How long had he been sitting there? For that matter, how long had he been walking across this prairie? How long ago was it that he had been standing on the crumbling river-bank, his back against the cottonwood, when he heard the cough and looked down into the eyes of the Indian? Only one, two, three—four days?

He remembered being so tired he had to think about every step and he seemed to be separated from himself. Now he felt separated in a different way, as if he were looking back at someone else across a stretch of time as big as the prairie he had been traveling.

It was almost black dark when Sequoyah stood up.

"Stay close," he said. Calvin nodded, realized that the Indian couldn't see him in the dark and smiled at himself, downwardly, in the Indian way.

Going up the hill, Sequoyah was a darker blackness ahead of him, and a rustle of grass. Calvin kept his eyes down, trying to see where he put his feet. At the top the Indian's stretched-out arm stopped him. He cupped his hand around Calvin's ear and whispered, "Wait here."

His shadow drifted away. Calvin hesitated a moment and then hurried after him and whispered, "Here, take the rifle." The Indian didn't say anything. In the darkness Calvin could imagine his smile. He held the rifle out. The Indian took it and was gone.

Calvin was alone. He felt his way to a clump of twisted bushes and sat down in the deeper darkness under them, his back against the springy stalks. The prairie emptiness was growing inside him. The darkness seemed to press against his eyeballs, making dancing yellow spots and then the idiot face of the yellow grasshopper, growing bigger and plainer as he thought about how alone he was.

He looked along the rim of the hill. The limbs of the bush overhead. Stars. A lighter spot in the sky to his left that promised a moon.

Now he could hear sounds. Field mice rustling the grass. A coyote. A faint squeaking somewhere—a bat, this far out on the prairie?

He stretched out his legs. No one could come up that hill and surprise him here in the deep shadows. And just by looking at the stars and the bushes and the other real things he could keep the face of the grasshopper away.

Dew began to gather in the night air, and he licked his lips with a leathery tongue. When he first heard the sound he sat still, listening. As it came closer he recognized the slip-step of Sequoyah's limp. The sliver of a moon was spreading a pale light over the hillside now, and when Calvin crawled out from under the bushes and stood up he could see the old man turn toward him. He was walking carelessly upright, and holding something in front of him.

"Here," he said as he came up. Calvin reached for what he supposed was the rifle, but he touched the brass kettle. It felt moist. "Drink it slowly," the Indian said.

Water. Calvin could taste the first gulp all the way down, opening up a new way into his insides. When he stopped for a breath, he asked, "Who made the smoke?"

The Indian slipped his blanket roll off his shoulder and dropped it. "Comanche," he said. Calvin stopped the kettle halfway to his lips. "A big camp," the old man went on. "They are gone now. The smoke was from old fires, very many. But the Comanche are gone."

"Where did you find the water?"

"A big stream in that valley. It tastes like spring water from the hills. The Comanche had camped there."

Calvin drained the kettle. "Let's get some more," he said.

The Indian slipped off his blanket roll. "We can wait until daybreak. In the morning we will find a place to make a camp where we can hunt a little and rest."

"All right. But don't bed down here. I found a place under some bushes over there."

"Lead the way," the Indian said.

As he walked toward the shadow of the bushes Calvin tried those words to himself. "Lead the way." He smiled in the dark.

NINE

Water

CALVIN JERKED awake in the half-light, his blanket clammy with dew. Ground fog swirled around Sequoyah, so that he seemed to be bending down out of a cloud—or out of heaven, in a dream—to shake Calvin's shoulder.

They waded out of a lake of wet smoke onto the bald ridge.

Sequoyah stopped. "How much land does your father own?" he asked, handing Calvin the rifle as he unwrapped what was left of the tongue they had roasted last night.

"About a section. A little over a section."

"Is that a lot?"

"That's a good-sized spread," Calvin said.

"As much as all this?" Sequoyah made one of his big gestures, moving his hand just a little, as he gave some of the cold meat to Calvin.

"Oh, no, not near this big."

"We own all this, this morning," Sequoyah said.

Calvin looked around. They stood on the very edge of the prairie. Down the slope ahead were trees, growing straight with limbs that were level, not twisted in an agony of thirst like the prairie scrub brush behind them. The breeze freshened, twisting wisps of fog into eddies and currents and carving liquid shapes in the buffalo grass. In the trees ahead a bird tried his morning voice.

They stepped off the edge into limp grass, letting the slope pull them along into the trees, faster as they went deeper until, glancing back, Calvin could not see the edge of the prairie any more.

Suddenly Sequoyah stopped.

Calvin dropped to one knee and swung the rifle up cocking it—*crick-crack-crick* loud in the silence—as it came level. He held his breath and tried to swallow his heart out of his throat.

"So that's how they do it," Sequoyah said softly.

Calvin thought about the Comanche way of hanging prisoners over a slow fire to watch them wiggle. Sequoyah motioned to him.

"What do you see?" Calvin asked.

"Look. Here's how they get the first one over."

Calvin stood up and took two quiet steps to come alongside the Indian, his hands wet on the rifle.

"See?" Sequoyah said, pointing to a swaying horseweed in front of them.

A black and yellow corn spider was standing somehow as if on tiptoe, almost at Calvin's eye level. "What do you—"

Calvin started, and then the morning breeze stirred and he saw what the Indian meant. A single wisp of web drifted away from the horseweed, seeming to stretch as the spider spun it out into the breeze, and as they watched, the free end touched a drooping tree limb and stuck. The spider tested it and then started across, upside down and swaying wildly, spinning another strand behind.

"He just starts making web," Sequoyah said, "and wherever it lands, there is the other end." He looked at Calvin and smiled. "Don't you remember?"

Calvin eased the hammer of the rifle back down and laughed, in spite of himself. "I remember," he said. "But right now I'm thirsty."

They walked around the beginning of the web and went on, side by side now. A covey of quail exploded under their feet, leaving a single curled underfeather hanging in the air like an echo. Calvin grabbed it, blew it off the palm of his hand and then ran to catch it again, making a game of walking.

As the slope flattened out, he paused half a step and sniffed. The fish-and-weeds scent, like Snake Creek back home, tightened his dry throat. Sequoyah was walking faster now, head bobbing with his limp, as they came out of the trees into reeds and grass that scattered seeds over their shoulders. Calvin looked up and down the valley, but all he saw was the wind shaping waves in the floppy reeds.

Something crashed through the cattails ahead of them, exploding pods into dandelion puffs, and then splashed away—a muskrat, or an otter perhaps. The sound made

Calvin drop the rifle and start running, stripping off his shirt then hobbling out of his pants and boots, the reeds and water grass whipping itchy welts across his thighs as he splashed through the shallows, chasing little green frogs ahead of him in squeaking leaps, until he felt the bottom slope out from under his feet and then he belly flopped into the cold middle, choking as he tried to drink and swim at the same time.

After he splashed and gasped, drank and dived, he floated a long time face down, watching the silver minnow flashes against the brown pebbles on the bottom, blowing slow bubbles through his nose and then raising his head like a turtle to suck another chestful of air. Everything inside him unhooked and relaxed.

Finally he stood up, treading water, and looked around for Sequoyah. Open water, grass, reeds, trees and shade. A dragonfly and one solemn blue crane, standing one-legged in the shallows. Silence. He paddled over to the reeds, called, and listened. He heard only the morning breeze that pebbled his wet skin with gooseflesh. He sloshed to the edge, feeling the bottom turn from rocks to mud under his feet as he waded through the lilies and water grass, and followed the trail of his scattered clothes, drying himself on his shirt. When he came to the place he had left the rifle, it was gone.

He was gooseflesh all over now. He made himself walk a slow circle, parting the grass with the boots he still carried, looking for the rifle and trying not to see the dense early shadows under the trees, which now seemed to be crawling down the hill toward him in the silence.

He found a pattern of bent grass that could be where the rifle had landed. He looked around once to put the shadows back in their place and then began to climb into his clothes. As he kicked a damp foot into a boot, he stirred up a single yellow grasshopper that sailed away at an angle as if looking back over its shoulder at him.

What had Sequoyah said about the Comanche camp? Many fires. He looked around for smoke, but saw nothing except the bloody glare of the sunrise reflected off the river.

Then he heard it, the ripping, retching sound of someone being sick. He turned and listened until it came again, nearby, close to the water. He ran toward the sound, calling, "Sequoyah?"

Something stirred the drooping whips of a willow at the water's edge, and so he angled that way, his bootheels clumping quietly into the soft ground. As he reached the screen of leaves he called again, and he heard Sequoyah say, "Wait."

He stopped, breathing hard and sucking in his own stomach at the sound of another spasm of retching. Finally Sequoyah, sounding far away, said, "Now come."

Calvin dropped to his knees and crawled through the trembling leaves. The Indian was sitting with his back against the trunk, the rifle beside him. He had taken off his turban. As Calvin watched he leaned over on one elbow, wet the red-and-yellow calico turban in the dark water that reached almost to the trunk, and mopped his face. As his eyes adjusted to the shade, Calvin noticed that Sequoyah's hair was completely white.

"The water tasted good," he said, smiling in his downward way, "but it was too big a surprise for my insides."

"I'm sorry," Calvin said, his voice cracking. "I didn't realize. I wasn't thinking about anything except how dry I was."

The Indian let his head drop back against the tree and closed his eyes, speaking so low that Calvin leaned forward to hear him. "We can rest here a few days. You can shoot some meat and maybe you can find some honey." He paused, as if catching his breath, and then went on. "Maybe Tessee and the Worm will find us here. Or maybe, after a few days, I will be able to go on again. If not, there is something you must do for me."

Calvin noticed that the water from the turban glistened in the pattern of tiny wrinkles in the Indian's face, and he thought again of the worn leather of the Bible cover, remembering how he had first thought that this man was Moses or Abraham coming out of a fever dream. He looked now like a man who had lived forever.

Sequoyah picked up a twig and scratched a twisted shape in the damp ground. "Here," he said, handing the twig to Calvin. "Learn to make that."

"I've seen that," Calvin said as he copied the mark. "I can't remember where, but I've seen it."

"That was my sign. I was a smith, and that was my sign. The Cherokee will know it. Some of the whites know it too, because I lived at the edge of the two worlds. But all the Cherokee will know it. I stamped it in everything I made. Silver and iron, tools and jewelry."

"Now I remember. It was on the buckles of the saddlebags in your cave. Did you make those?"

The Indian nodded. "I traded hides and corn for silver and iron. Then I hammered the silver into buckles and bracelets, and the iron into hinges and tools. I traded them to the Cherokee for more corn and hides. Back and forth between the two worlds."

Calvin smiled and shook his head. "I thought you must have stolen those saddlebags."

The Indian nodded. "Because I am Indian. The Cherokee didn't trust me either, because I am white."

"White?"

"Half white. To you I am Indian. To them I am white. On the edge of two worlds. And where two worlds meet, they make a lonely place."

"What do you want me to do?" Calvin asked.

"When the time comes, I will tell you. Maybe nothing. Maybe Tessee and the Worm will find us. But remember the mark. If you must do it, the mark will say that you really come from me. The Cherokee all know my mark."

Calvin erased the mark with his hand and then drew it again, over and over, until he could make it with a single stroke.

TEN

The Turtle

THE NEXT day Calvin started out early, while one bullfrog was still burping his night song in the mist-smoky shallows below the willow where they had camped.

"Scout the valley well before you shoot," Sequoyah said. "And watch for bees."

He seemed smaller this morning, as if his illness had shrunk him overnight. Last night he had been too sick even for soup. Calvin had built another fire up the hillside where he could feast on buffalo steak alone. He had trimmed the fat from the tough, beefy meat and rubbed it on his water-cracked boots until the leather was black and almost soft again. Some of the meat he had saved to warm over the gray coals for breakfast, and a small piece he carried now in his hip pocket.

The long drink of river water gurgled a little inside him,

and his greased boots made a comfortable squeak as he climbed fast in the cool morning sunshine.

As he approached the edge of the prairie where the slope was steeper and the trees grew smaller and twisted, Calvin climbed slower. He stopped at the bald ridge that had been an island in the fog yesterday morning. Now, looking down the slope, he could pick out the stunted bushes where he had waited for Sequoyah, and below them the prairie. Had they really walked that whole stretched-out yellow and brown distance?

Back the other way the slope plunged into trees. Two worlds: one, tumbleweed, buffalo grass and a dry wind; the other, trees, water hyacinths and a shallow river shivering over the gravel bar. Calvin could still hear Sequoyah saying, "Where two worlds meet they make a lonely place."

The shadow of a hawk skated by and all around him the birds hushed. He hadn't heard their twittering, but now he heard the silence. He raised the rifle and looked around.

Down below he saw a turtle sprawled on the surface of the pool where Calvin had turtle-floated himself the day before. He looked back at the world of tumbleweed and buffalo grass one more time, and then he started down again. He didn't let himself run. Among the big trees the birds were singing.

When he got to the pool the turtle was gone. Calvin sat on his heels and waited. He tried holding his own breath to measure the time, and he had to refill once, again, and once more before he saw the horny snout poke through the surface again downstream.

Calvin hid the rifle in the grass, looking around quickly to mark the place by a lightning-scarred cottonwood nearby, while he kept watching the bull's-eye of ripples circling the turtle's snout. He pulled the tomahawk out of his belt so that he could run better and started along the edge of the river, dodging in and out through the willows, half bent over to stay hidden.

The turtle dived, but Calvin could run faster than the turtle swam with the slow current. He stopped once to pick up a fallen hickory limb. The turtle grounded against the gravel bar and started clambering across. Calvin splashed out on the bar and headed him off. The turtle squeezed back into his shell, and Calvin pried him over on his back with the limb. He grabbed the scaly tail but let go when the turtle hissed like a snake.

Using the limb, he half rolled, half slid the turtle along the gravel bar. After a few feet the neck snaked out and the parrot beak grabbed the limb. Calvin hung on and pulled him up onto the bank.

The turtle let Calvin stretch his neck out for the toma-hawk. Calvin had to take two whacks. The turtle blinked once and stiffened his legs, but when Calvin threw the stick into the bushes the head was still hooked to it.

He shuddered once, glad Sequoyah was not there to see him, and then turned the heavy shell up on edge. Using the ax as a wedge, he split it apart into two shallow bowls, each bigger than his mother's Sunday platter. Inside were only a few scraps of guts between flippers, neck and tail.

He carried the meat back to camp in one shell, and the Indian helped him peel off the leathery skin.

"I heard you splashing," he said. "I thought you were catching fish."

"This river looks like good fishing," Calvin said, "but we don't have hooks and line."

"I could show you how to catch them the Cherokee way."

"How?"

"Just find a quiet pool and throw in a lot of green walnut hulls."

"Green walnut hulls?"

"They bring the fish up. Right up to the top. Green walnut hulls do to fish what whiskey does to Indians."

Calvin laughed. "I'd like to try that."

"The fishing or the whiskey?" The old man laughed with him. "I've tried both, and for me the fishing is better. But right now, this turtle will be better than fish for me." He held up a double handful of slippery white meat. "It would take a barrel of turtles to make a bowl of meat, though."

Calvin washed his hands in the river and then filled the brass kettle. He built up the fire and put the meat on to boil. After it had simmered down into a thick soup, he set it off to cool. Sequoyah sipped a little first, and then nodded and handed the kettle to Calvin. It tasted rich, wild and strong, needing salt, but so good that Calvin had to be careful not to take more than his share.

Sequoyah drank a little that afternoon and more that

night. Afterward he seemed stronger. He sat up against the willow tree, writing in the narrow ledger. Calvin watched the strange characters taking shape under the thin hand as the fire burned down to a feathery gray heap.

Finally he asked, "Are you writing about why you came down here?"

"In a way, yes." He closed the book. "We have heard about a Cherokee band that lived in Texas. The whites chased them out, just like us. But these they drove into Mexico."

"Where did they come from?" Calvin asked. "I mean originally?"

"I don't know. We don't know where the Cherokee came from to the Echota country either. Before me there was no writing, and so we have only the stories that were passed on from man to boy. The stories say the Cherokee came from a land of lakes far to the north. The Senecas called us cave people because they said we came out of the ground in the mountains of the mists. But no one knows."

Calvin looked up at the nighthawks wheeling and darting in the gathering dusk. A cicada drummed monotonously overhead. "Is it so important? I mean where they came from. I don't know where my people started out, exactly."

"Maybe not," Sequoyah said. "Who knows what is important? Beginnings seem important to old men." He sipped the last of the turtle soup, tapping the kettle to get the meat. "It's an idea that took hold of me. You know— like how does a spider start his web, or how to make a talking leaf for the Cherokee. Where did they come from? Someplace out here in the plains, maybe?"

"Maybe. What if they did?"

"The Cherokee build houses," the old man said, his voice louder. "We don't roll up skin tents and ride away like the Comanche. We build houses of logs and raise maize and squash and beans. We don't change things either, like the whites. The world seems right to us the way it is. We are part of where we are. A place is important."

"You mean the houses and things?"

Sequoyah made one of his slight, big gestures. "The whole place. Mountains, streams, the river—the Cherokee country was where the *Nunnehi* lived."

"What are they—spirits?"

"They were warriors that could shoot around corners. They came out of the rocks when the Cherokee needed help."

"Do you believe that?"

"I never actually saw them. But I was at Horseshoe Bend, with your General Jackson, and I saw a band of Cherokee chase an army of Creeks out of the Cherokee country."

He stood up and started spreading out his blanket for the night. "Is that what you're writing?" Calvin asked, arranging his own bed.

"No, Echota is not Cherokee country anymore. I'm writing about—out here. About the first Cherokee. Before we went to Echota."

"Out here?"

The Indian nodded. "If there is a Cherokee band out here, maybe they were descended from the first Cherokee. Maybe this is really Cherokee country. Not just Echota, but out here too."

"Are you writing something for me to take back to the Cherokee? I mean, if you . . ."

"I'm trying to write it. But we are not yet a writing people. Even for me, some things tell better than they read. When I try to write everything out, the meaning gets lost in the words. In the explaining."

Calvin nodded. "Some things tell better than they read in any language, I guess."

"You may have to tell it for me, then," Sequoyah said.

"I can't do that. I don't even understand it myself."

"Maybe it's better that way. You understand that I am looking for our beginnings. Out here the Cherokee feel like strangers, but I think maybe this is really Cherokee country."

"Do you mean here in Texas?"

Sequoyah shrugged. "Texas, Mexico, Arkansas—that doesn't matter. What matters is out here, in the West, away from Echota. If Tessee and the Worm don't find us, just tell them about that, and you won't lose the meaning in a lot of other words." He rolled over with his back to the fire. "Just tell them about the Cherokee country out here. That is the only important part."

ELEVEN

Two Feathers

THE NEXT day Calvin followed the river past the riffle where he had caught the turtle. At the bend was a flat meadow where the river probably made a shortcut every spring and drowned any trees that had tried to get started. Now the meadow was a shimmering mass of brown-eyed Susans so bright they made the river look blue as it bent around them. Beyond that cheerful orange stood a few bare lodgepoles of the Comanche camp, reaching their bony shadows toward him across the blooms.

Calvin sat down on a rock, holding the rifle in both hands, looking at the lodgepoles. Why had the Comanche left them? Were they coming back to this place?

The sun was high, now, and hot, but Calvin shivered. He could see that one of the lodgepoles was broken. Probably these were poles that had been dragged too long behind the mustang ponies and so the Comanche had cut new ones in the timber here to replace them.

Calvin knew there was nothing dangerous in a dozen deserted lodgepoles, but after a while he stood up and followed the river back the other way. He came to a narrow trickle of water spilling down from the hills into the river and followed it, climbing up to the mossy spring where the trickle began. He drank, chewing the water to get all the rocky, deep earth taste that made him think of the well in the pasture at home. Then he sat down under a pin-oak tree with the rifle across his lap.

A shadow passed over. He looked around in time to see a big bird flare its wings and land lightly in a sumac thicket below the spring. Calvin blinked and the bird was gone.

Was it a hawk, or an eagle? It had landed, not struck. A buzzard? No, it had dropped into the underbrush deftly as a quail.

A turkey, maybe. Slowly, slowly he raised the rifle. He put his elbows on his knees, squinting to see into the sumac thicket. After a long time the bird took a slow step that revealed its shape in the mottled pattern of shadows. Aiming downhill, Calvin remembered the antelope and sighted low. As his finger tightened on the trigger, he thought of the Comanche camp and hesitated.

Silently he told himself, "It's empty," and then he fired.

The sumac thicket exploded. Limbs thrashed and leaves scattered. Calvin could hear three separate gunshot echoes coming back from the hills. He sat still a long time after everything was quiet again, feeling eyes everywhere, before he could get up and walk down to the thicket.

The dead turkey looked huddled and small in the brush, but when he gathered up the yellow, hook-clawed feet and lifted it, the wings flopped out wider than he could reach. He hoisted it across his shoulders, the wattled beak almost touching the ground behind him, and started back along the ridge.

When he came into the camp, Sequoyah stood up and took a step to meet him. He examined the turkey for a moment without saying anything, spreading the stiff wing feathers to show the bands of white, black and bronze. Then he said, "May I have one of the feathers of your kill?"

Calvin said, "What? Sure."

The Indian selected a long plume and carefully worked it loose. He smoothed it between his fingers and then stuck it in the fold of his turban.

"Now I will help you with the squaw work," he said.

Calvin held the turkey's legs while Sequoyah slit each one between tendon and shin, just behind the horny spur. Then he cut a thumb-sized willow shoot, shaved it smooth and slipped it through the slits. Using it as a handle, Calvin hung the stiffening turkey over a low limb.

He started jerking out the wing quills while Sequoyah was stripping the ridged breast. As he worked Calvin glanced out the sides of his eyes at the plume in Sequoyah's turban. When he pulled another perfect feather, Calvin stuck it in the band of his own hat. Sequoyah looked around and nodded.

Sequoyah opened the cavity carefully to save the gizzard, liver and heart, which he started simmering in the brass kettle while Calvin cut green forked stakes to make a spit.

Calvin roasted the bird whole, turning it slowly while his stomach twisted at the smell of the fat sizzling in the coals.

Sequoyah sat beside him, sipping the hot soup from the kettle.

"Did you see any bees?"

"No. I looked, but I didn't see any."

"Where did you hunt?"

"Back there."

"Along the river?"

"No, back there along the ridge."

"You're not apt to find a bee tree up there."

"Why not?"

"Not many flowers probably."

Calvin didn't say anything. He stared into the throbbing orange heart of the fire, seeing the field of orange flowers around the Comanche camp. He remembered how the shadows of the lodgepoles had reached toward him.

Finally, without looking at Sequoyah, he said, "Was there ever anything you were afraid of? I mean, for no good reason."

"Everyone is afraid of things."

"I mean, things that you know can't hurt you. Like, say, grasshoppers. I hate grasshoppers."

Sequoyah nodded. "Everyone is afraid of things. Sometimes the difference between men is which things they are afraid of."

Calvin looked at the flowers in the fire. A gobbet of fat dropped and sputtered, smelling like Christmas. Finally he said, "Tomorrow I'll find a bee tree."

TWELVE

Buffalo Hunters

THE SMELL of the crushed grass reminded Calvin of hay-lofts and cows' breath. Lying on his back, he looked through bending grass that stretched toward the sky. The clouds seemed to be crawling over the hairy seed caps, making each stem nod and spring back.

Calvin tried to remember what Sequoyah had said about the way the Cherokee see things. The deer, the woods, the streams and the Cherokee, all parts of the same thing. Buffalo, wolves and people. Right now, when the sky looked so close that the clouds brushed grass, Calvin could understand that idea. The clouds jumped back up into the sky as he sat up to look around again.

Tenderly he touched the four throbbing bee stings on his face. Earlier he had blown smoke into the bee tree until he was dizzy, but fresh bees had kept coming from the blooming meadow. When two hit him in the face at once he had almost fallen, and as he scrambled down, another had speared him clear through his pants. They chased him into the river.

Remembering Sequoyah on the day after the storm, Calvin had daubed wet clay on the stings, streaking his face with long smears to soak out the burning. Then he had settled down on the ridge to wait until dusk, when all the bees should be inside, to try again.

He dreaded the thought of sticking his face into that nest of hot points again, but he wasn't going back to camp this time without the honey.

He looked around at the two worlds, glanced at the sun— maybe two hours left before dusk—and lay down again in the grass. He crushed a sappy stem under his nose.

The smell of cut grass. His father could lay down a swath as wide as a wagon bed with each two-handed stroke of the big scythe. The blade made a musical sound—*thrang!*— and sometimes half-grown rabbits darted out into the stubble just ahead of it. Calvin closed his eyes, and he was back home at hay time.

At the far end of the meadow, where the hay had been down curing in the sun for a day, the wagon went back and forth. Two men followed, forking the yellowing hay onto the load as the team plodded along—step and pause, step and pause—with the harness reins dangling loose beside their heads.

Already there were too many things Calvin couldn't remember about home, but now with meadow smells and sounds all around him he could almost see that team. They were matched dappled grays, with broad backs, patient eyes, curious ears and long cuffs of gray hair above each hoof. Sometimes they cheated, twisting sideways to steal a mouthful of hay. Calvin could even hear the *scrunch, scrunch* of the horses chewing.

He jerked awake. There it was again—*scrunch, scrunch*—the sound of a horse ripping grass.

Calvin rolled over on his belly. Off to his right he heard a thud—a horse stamping flies away from his ankles. Very carefully, Calvin raised his head to look down the hillside. They were so close he dropped down again and lay still, listening.

Only horse noises. He made himself think one thing at a time. Three horses. How many riders? Two, at least. In his mind's eye he could see the horses, looking all head and shoulders as they climbed toward him from the river side of the ridge, the first a bay, the next some other color and the third, a little farther back, white.

A white mule!

He felt for the rifle and then raised his head slowly again. There they were, so close now he could see the yellow moustache of the rider on the bay horse.

Calvin sat up. He remembered the other time—it seemed years ago—sitting on a bale of green hides in the wagon bed, watching the prairie dust puff turn into a single stretched-out spot, to three shapes, and then to two horses and a white mule. And one of the buffalo hunters had worn a yellow moustache.

Now Calvin was grinning so wide he couldn't say anything as the riders came on, heads down, following his trail up the slope. Calvin picked his hat out of the grass and put it on as he stood up. Yellow Moustache raised his head.

When he was little, Calvin had played wooden soldiers in bed. He would arrange them in charging positions, facing up the slope of covers. Then, manning an imaginary cannon at the top of a bedclothes mountain, he would yell, "Boom!" twitching the blankets, and the soldiers would topple over backward.

Now when he stood up at the top of the ridge it was as if he had twitched the blankets. The two buffalo hunters reared back in their saddles, hauling the reins so short that the horses sat back on their haunches and pawed the air as they skidded downhill and then crashed over on their sides, while the white mule snorted and veered down the slope, bucking off his canvas-wrapped packs as he ran.

Pots and pans crash-banged down the slope. Yellow Moustache threw one leg over his saddle horn and dived off, his slouch hat marking in empty air the place he had been when Calvin twitched the blankets. The other hunter held on to the saddle horn, bootheels up alongside his horse's ears, and then hopped off just as the horse went over, his momentum taking him, elbows pumping, down the slope a few leaps before he tripped and belly flopped in the weeds.

Silence. Even one of the horses stopped, turned around and looked at Calvin. He swallowed twice, and said, "I'm sorry."

More silence. Calvin noticed that Yellow Moustache was pointing a buffalo gun at him. He looked down the slope into the barrel of another. "Look, I'm sorry. I didn't mean to. I was just glad to see you, that's all."

The hunters looked at each other. "It's a white boy," Yellow Moustache said.

"Of course I'm—" Calvin began. "Don't you remember me? You camped with us. Back on the prairie."

"Remember that kid on the freight wagons?" the down-hill hunter said.

"That's right. That's who I am."

Yellow Moustache lowered the muzzle. He cocked his head like a bird, squinting uphill. "I was within a hair of giving you a slug. What are you doing way off down here around an Injun village wearing a feather in your hat and war paint on your face?"

Calvin raised his hand and touched the crumbling streaks of clay on his face. Before he could stop he laughed out loud. "I got bee-stung. The Comanche shot up our wagons. They killed the drivers."

"What's so funny about that?"

"Oh, that's not—look, everything's all mixed up. Aren't you going to catch that mule before he runs all the way to Mexico?"

Yellow Moustache twisted around and swore. The mule was a white patch in the trees by the river now, slowed down to a trot but still going. "I'll see if I can head him off," he said, getting to his feet and hobbling after his horse. "Make this kid help you pick up our truck. Maybe you can find a reason to boot him all the way down the hill."

THIRTEEN

Decision

"THERE USED to be some Cherokee around here," the buffalo hunter said, whipping the coffee grounds out of his cup into the fire. His two front teeth were broken off at the gums, and the thought occurred to Calvin that in some trading post town there was probably a man with scarred knuckles.

Calvin stretched out his legs, trying to find a way to sit that didn't hurt either his bee stings or the new sore spots carved by the sawtooth spine of the white mule he had been riding through the dusk and into the night until the buffalo hunters finally stopped.

"I hunted through here in '35," the man with the broken teeth went on, "and traded with some Cherokee for hides. They lived along the Neches River in regular houses, almost like people." He refilled his cup and then broke open his jack-o'-lantern grin. "I remember they had peach trees. With big, fuzzy soft peaches."

"Do they take live prisoners, like this one did?" Yellow Moustache asked.

"I don't know," Jack-o'-lantern said. "When I traded with them they was peaceful as farmers. Matter of fact, they *was* farmers. Some of them had cattle. But not long after that I heard about a big hoorah with the Texans. The way I heard it, the Cherokee got burned out and run clear across the Rio Grande into Mexico. I've often wondered if those peach trees got burned up too."

"If they got chased across the river," Yellow Moustache said, "then I wonder what this one's doing warpathing up here by hisself and taking white prisoners."

"He didn't really take me prisoner," Calvin tried to explain. "At least, not after the first day."

"You're a lucky young'un," Yellow Moustache said. "I saw what was left of some Apache prisoners one time, and I can tell you I'd rather be fourteen times dead than once an Injun prisoner."

"I've been lucky all around," Calvin said. His head was so full of home—the springhouse, Mother and Father, swimming in the creek, Shep—that he couldn't fish out anything that said how he felt. "And lucky you crossed my trail—you must have circled back. Did you find my message? The hunters looked at each other. Calvin noticed that these two understood each other so well they talked almost as much with glances and gestures as they did with words. The way he and Sequoyah—he put that thought out of his mind.

"What message?" Yellow Moustache said.

"I left a sign back on the trail. You know—calling for help."

"You mean, in writing?"

Calvin nodded. "Just marked on a tree."

The hunters glanced at each other again, and Jack-o'-lantern grinned. "We can't neither one of us read writing, boy, but we can read trail sign. We've been up ahead there, wandering around after the herd. When we came back to the river to water our stock we read your bootheels stomped in the mud to say there was a lone white man afoot in this Injun country."

Calvin nodded. "I *was* alone for a while. But then I joined up with this Indian, and he was leaving regular letters behind."

"What kind of letters?"

"Regular writing, only in Cherokee."

"What are you talking about?" Yellow Moustache said. "Do you mean picture talk?"

"No, regular writing. Just like ours. He even used some of our letters, only he gave them Cherokee sounds." Calvin saw the two hunters exchange a look again, and so he didn't say any more.

Jack-o'-lantern said, "Don't I remember you said your pa runs a spread back on the Snake Creek?" Calvin nodded. "We'll be trailing through that country on our way back north, after we get a load of hides. I reckon your pa will be right glad to see you."

"He'll be glad to see me, all right," Calvin said. "And for a while I didn't think he ever would again." He looked away, doodling in the dust with his finger. After a moment he realized he had traced Sequoyah's mark.

"Say, before we go on, would you mind letting me take care of something?"

"What do you mean?" Yellow Moustache said.

"Just something I'd like to do before I leave here. Won't take me long—half a day, maybe."

Yellow Moustache shook his head. "We've got to catch up to that herd. We're moving out at first light in the morning."

"What have you got to do, boy?" Jack-o'-lantern asked.

"Well, you see I have his rifle. The least I could do . . . It's not important, I guess."

The two hunters exchanged another look. "Are you talking about that Injun that took you prisoner?" Yellow Moustache said.

"I wasn't a prisoner, really. And he's an old man. And sick."

"Could you lead us to him?"

This time Calvin understood their look. He didn't answer, and finally Jack-o'-lantern said, "That's a two or three hour ride back to the river where we found this kid. If we don't get after those buffler we'll never get any more hides."

Yellow Moustache didn't answer for a moment, and then he said, "I guess so. Seems a shame, though, if the boy could take us right to him. It's like leaving a treed cat."

Calvin didn't say anything. Nighthawks darted and swooped above them and the firelight drew moths to fly death-dares above the flames.

"He's treed in heavy cover, though," Jack-o'-lantern

said. "I'd just as soon have a rattlesnake treed in my own coatsleeves as a Comanche in tall timber."

"He's not a Comanche," Calvin said. "He's a Cherokee."

"He's an Injun."

"If there's a good breeze in the morning we might could burn him out," Yellow Moustache said. "These cedars would burn like fat, and the brush is pretty dry."

Calvin stood up. "He's just an old man."

The two hunters looked at him, and then at each other. Finally Jack-o'-lantern said, "Sit down, boy. You'll feel better after you get a night's sleep. And before long you'll be with your own folks again."

"I've got to go back," Calvin said quietly.

"We're taking you back, just as soon as we load up with hides."

"No, I mean back to him. He helped me. Now . . . I just have to go back, that's all."

The two hunters stood up. "What's the matter with him?" Yellow Moustache said.

Jack-o'-lantern shook his head. "I saw a little girl once who had been captured. When we got her back from the Apache all she did was sit and look straight in front of her all day. Didn't cry or smile or say nothing. Brain-scalded, like a rabbit watching a weasel, too scared to move. This boy's likely had a powerful scare too."

"You don't understand," Calvin said. "That's the way I was at first. Everything was scared out of me. But now . . . but he . . . Look, I can't explain it."

Neither of the hunters moved.

Calvin tried again. "I really do appreciate what you tried

to do for me. I thank you for that, and I'd like to go home with you. I really would. But don't you see, he's an old man. He's always had to do everything himself. Great things— all by himself. But now . . . now there's something I might have to help him do."

Yellow Moustache edged around the circle of firelight toward him, and Calvin backed away a step. "That white mule," Calvin said. "He can't be worth a whole lot. I've got sixty dollars of American money—I'll give you all of it for that mule."

Yellow Moustache took another step forward and Calvin took another backward. "Sixty dollars is worth a lot of hides," he said. "Are you sure you won't . . . I guess not." He grabbed his rifle. Yellow Moustache picked up his own rifle at the same time.

"Boy, that mule is the only pack animal we've got left," Jack-o'-lantern said from across the fire. "All our others are puffed up dead from bad water back there, along with our wagons. We've got hides hid out now that we can't pack until we get a chance to trade with the Mexicans for horses."

"Just let me go, then," Calvin said. "I'll be all right, and you can go on after the buffalo."

"Put the rifle down, boy," Jack-o'-lantern said, "and come on over here by the fire. We'll have some meat roasting in a minute and then you'll feel better."

Calvin shook his head. "I'm going," he said. "Don't try to stop me."

"Is that any way to do," Jack-o'-lantern said. "After

we've rescued you from that Injun, is that any way to do? Now, come on."

"No. Thank you. No." Calvin turned and walked away.

"Stop, boy!"

Calvin looked back. Yellow Moustache had the buffalo gun leveled at him. Calvin turned around.

"You wouldn't shoot me?"

Yellow Moustache nodded. "Before I'd let a crazy boy run off to the Injuns I would. I'd knock his leg out and then carry him back to his people tied over the back of that mule. Now come over here to the fire."

Calvin looked over to Jack-o'-lantern. He was still standing by the fire, his rifle leaning against his saddle. Calvin hesitated.

"I'm going on," he said finally. "If you shoot, that gun'll blow up in your face."

"What are you talking about?" Yellow Moustache said.

"I slipped a hickory switch down the muzzle of your rifle," Calvin said

No one moved. "I don't believe you," Yellow Moustache said.

"When you were hobbling the horses. I decided then I was going back. And now I'm going."

A log fell in the fire, sending up a fountain of sparks. In the light Calvin could see the rifle muzzle waver.

Jack-o'-lantern laughed quietly. "He's picked up some Injun tricks, ain't he?"

"I don't believe him," Yellow Moustache said. "I don't think he thought about going back until just now."

"You're probably right," Jack-o'-lantern said. "But I'd want to be sure."

Calvin took a step away.

Suddenly Yellow Moustache pointed the rifle down and shook it. Calvin ran. He headed toward the horses, sprinting hard to get them between him and the campfire. Behind him he could hear Jack-o'-lantern laugh and say, "You was right—nothing in there. That boy's a snaky one, ain't he?"

"Get the horses. Head him off," Yellow Moustache yelled. Calvin couldn't hear Jack-o'-lantern's answer. He ran along a low ridge, bent over to stay out of sight, until he was gasping for breath, and then he threw himself in the tall grass, crawled to the edge and looked back. He could just see the blurred shapes of the two hunters standing at the edge of the firelight. They were looking out across the prairie, not going to the horses. After a while the taller one, which he remembered was Jack-o'-lantern, took the other by the arm and led him back to the fire.

Calvin rolled over on his back and looked up at the stars. He was alone again, on the prairie. He laughed, softly at first, as he thought of Yellow Moustache shaking out his buffalo gun, and then louder. Let them hear. They could never find him now. He knew this prairie like an Indian.

FOURTEEN

Alone

CALVIN'S FATHER had shown him Job's coffin one summer night. It was a lopsided diamond of stars hanging over the adobe chimney of the ranch house. Now it was over the back trail of the buffalo hunters' horses, and Calvin followed it through the rustling dark.

Yes, he knew this prairie like an Indian—but he had gotten lost as soon as he tried to find his way back. He had spent half the night stumbling around in the dark trying to find the back trail. Even now he kept wondering if he were lost again, because the way back seemed so much longer on foot and in the dark than it had seemed riding the white mule.

Once a clump of weeds on a small rise shaped the line of the ranch house roof and chimney so perfectly that Calvin stopped and stared at it.

"I can't explain it to you," he said into the empty darkness as he walked on. "I just had to go back. It's like you had to come to Texas. You had a big white house back in Missouri, and Mother says people used to tip their hats to you and call you 'Judge.' But you had to leave and come to Texas. Well, I have to go back and help him."

The sun was rising as he went over the edge of the prairie down the slope into the trees. Just like the morning he and Sequoyah had first come to this edge of two worlds, he kicked up an explosion of quail, probably the same covey roosting in the same spot. But as soon as he came out onto the riverbank, calling, "Hallo!" to Sequoyah, he felt something was different.

He stopped and raised the rifle, looking around. A fire smoked in the circle of blackened rocks by the willow. Nearby was the scraped-out turtle shell. Beyond were the reeds and cattails, and beyond them the river, red with reflected sunrise.

Nothing moved. Somehow the silence was a hush, the kind of quiet that follows the shadow of a hawk across a hillside. Calvin's neck prickled with the touch of unseen eyes, as it had when Sequoyah left him alone on the raft.

A noise—the grunt-grumbling sound of Indian talk. Calvin swung the rifle up the hillside to his left toward the sound and dropped to one knee. An answering grunt-grumble from the right. As he swung back to face it, Calvin recognized that the answering voice was Sequoyah's. The screen of willow whips parted and Sequoyah stepped out.

"You've come back," he said. His voice seemed to come from a great distance, and Calvin could see him sway, his knees wobbling. Calvin looked back up the hillside toward the other voice.

"My son and the Worm found me," Sequoyah said. He said something in Cherokee, and two men stepped out of the woods and walked toward the fire. "They heard you coming down the hill and thought you might be . . ." He swayed again and sat down, one hand propped on the ground.

Calvin lowered the rifle and walked down to the fire. The other Indians were also wearing turbans and blousy cotton shirts. One was squat and muscular. The other had a face like Sequoyah's with sharp lines of bone along the nose, cheeks and jaw.

As Calvin came to the fire Sequoyah looked up and smiled. "They are here in time. They can help me now."

Calvin let the butt of the rifle slide to the ground and shook his head. "I walked all night," he said. "I was with the buffalo hunters. They were going to take me home. But . . . I walked all night to get back."

"Thank you for that," Sequoyah said.

Calvin shook his head slowly. He felt like an empty sack. He looked at the other two Indians and then back at Sequoyah. "They were going to take me home," he said again.

Sequoyah nodded. "I understand," he said. "Rest now, and then we will talk about it."

Calvin dozed while the two Indians roasted squirrels on green stick spits. He roused long enough to eat and then took his blanket into the shade and slept until afternoon. He woke slowly, with Sequoyah sitting beside him.

Calvin looked sleepily at him a moment and then he said, "You look better."

Sequoyah nodded. "The Worm brought bread. It is better for me than game."

"Did they find the Cherokee down there?"

"Yes."

"Do they have peach trees?"

"Peach trees?"

"One of the buffalo hunters told me that down there the Cherokee have peach trees. Or used to. Now that you know this is Cherokee country, do you still have to go all the way to Mexico?"

"Yes. There is still a little of me left, and I want to use it to go the rest of the way. After that, Tessee and the Worm can take the word back."

Calvin looked away. "What will they say—about why you came down here?"

Sequoyah shrugged. "Probably just that we found the Cherokee band—and that I am buried down here. That's enough. The people will find their own meanings in that. And whatever they find will turn their faces away from the East a little." He reached out and squeezed Calvin's shoulder. "But what about you?"

"I don't know," Calvin said.

"We have horses. We have food and a rifle for you. You could catch up with the buffalo hunters again. Or you could follow this river north. Tessee and the Worm say there is a white town only two days' ride from here. From there you could get home."

Calvin sat up. "Or from there I could join up with another wagon train."

Sequoyah smiled downwardly and nodded. "And go on to your school of laws," he said.

The next morning the pony kicked and danced in the chilly ground fog so that the two Indians had to hold him while Calvin hauled the saddle girths tight.

"He must smell rain," Calvin said, putting his foot in the horse's ribs to cinch the straps. "My pa says changes in the weather make cows hook and horses pitch. And kids sillier."

"Kids?" the Worm said, trying the word on his tongue.

"Children. He meant like me, when he said it."

"What did he say about Indians?"

Calvin laughed, avoiding an answer.

They led the horse to the river so that he could drink while they filled two big gourds and strung them behind the saddle with a rawhide strap. The pony's belly was so tight with meadow grass that he didn't want to drink at first, and so they waited.

"How long will you stay here?" Calvin said.

"Not long enough," Tessee answered. "He will want to go on as soon as he can ride."

"Don't leave him alone again," Calvin said.

Tessee shook his head. "Never. The Worm can take the word back. I will stay with him."

"There is a spring up there in the hills where the game comes in the evenings," Calvin said. "I wish I could hunt with you a while, but I have a long way to go."

"Where is your school?" Tessee asked.

"It's in a town called Boston. Farther even than Echota," Calvin said.

"I could go with you a ways," the Worm said.

Calvin shook his head. "I guess he gave me enough buffalo juice to make it alone." He swatted the horse's rump. "Drink, stubborn. We've got a lot of prairie to cross."

He looked down the river. Another turtle poked his horny snout through a bull's-eye of ripples. Sequoyah came out of the willow screen and stood waiting for them. Finally the horse drank, snorting and mouthing the top of the water as if he had just discovered it.

When he finished he stood quietly, but when Calvin swung into the saddle the pony jumped sideways, pitching and sunfishing. Calvin reined uphill to stop him, but the pony bucked into a gallop and plunged all the way to the top. When he reached the edge of the two worlds along the ridge his sides were heaving, so that Calvin could haul him up.

Calvin turned in the saddle and looked back. The three Indians were standing together by the willow. Calvin turned the pony around, but before he started down the slope Sequoyah waved. Calvin paused. He sat for a long moment looking down at them, and then he waved too and turned the pony toward the prairie.

The sun was up and there was no wind. As far as he could see across the stretched-out and sunburned world of Texas, the only thing that moved was a yellow grasshopper. Calvin looked around at the same toast-brown tufts of grass, the same yellow-freckled boulders with the same heat halo shimmering above them, and smiled downwardly, in the Indian way, feeling as if he owned it all.

Author's Note

IS IT TRUE?

Yes—as true as I could imagine it. Many of the ordinary things in the story are made up, but all the extraordinary things are facts.

Sequoyah is a fact. So is his walk halfway across Texas. So are Tessee and the Worm, the cave and the flood, the signal fires and the letters along the trail.

Jack-o'-lantern and Yellow Moustache are not facts, but they are true—true as the catfish, the turkey, the grasshoppers and the other things that lived in the Texas of that time. The Cherokee trip from Echota in the Great Smoky Mountains to the foothills of the Ozarks is a fact. Sequoyah went with one of the first parties. Most of the Cherokee came later, driven out of their mountains by United States soldiers. Winter caught them and thousands died along what they came to call the Trail of Tears.

140

The most unlikely part of the story is the Sequoyah alphabet, but here that is:

Ꭰ a	Ꭱ e	Ꭲ i	Ꭳ o	Ꭴ u	Ꭵ v
Ꭶ ga Ꭷ ka	Ꭸ ge	Ꭹ gi	Ꭺ go	Ꭻ gu	Ꭼ gv
Ꭽ ha	Ꭾ he	Ꭿ hi	Ꮀ ho	Ꮁ hu	Ꮂ hv
Ꮃ la	Ꮄ le	Ꮅ li	Ꮆ lo	Ꮇ lu	Ꮈ lv
Ꮉ ma	Ꮊ me	Ꮋ mi	Ꮌ mo	Ꮍ mu	
Ꮎ na	Ꮑ ne	Ꮒ ni	Ꮓ no	Ꮔ nu	Ꮕ nv
Ꮏ hna	Ꮐ nah				
Ꮖ kwa	Ꮗ kwe	Ꮘ kwi	Ꮙ kwo	Ꮚ kwu	Ꮛ kwv
Ꮜ sa Ꮝ s	Ꮞ se	Ꮟ si	Ꮠ so	Ꮡ su	Ꮢ sv
Ꮣ da	Ꮥ de	Ꮧ di	Ꮩ do	Ꮪ du	Ꮫ dv
Ꮤ ta	Ꮦ te	Ꮨ ti			
Ꮬ dla Ꮭ tla	Ꮮ tle	Ꮯ tli	Ꮰ tlo	Ꮱ tlu	Ꮲ tlv
Ꮳ tsa	Ꮴ tse	Ꮵ tsi	Ꮶ tso	Ꮷ tsu	Ꮸ tsv
Ꮹ wa	Ꮺ we	Ꮻ wi	Ꮼ wo	Ꮽ wu	Ꮾ wv
Ꮿ ya	Ᏸ ye	Ᏹ yi	Ᏺ yo	Ᏻ yu	Ᏼ yv

Egyptian, Roman, Arabic, Hebrew and all the other written languages must have grown, like speech, from simple to more complex forms over hundreds of years. Sequoyah, an illiterate thirty-six-year-old silversmith, boasted over a hunting fire, "This is very easy. I can do it myself." And he did.

First he tried to make a picture for each sound in the language. This was too complicated and so he tried signs, one for every word. A year and several thousand different signs later, he decided this was also too complicated. He didn't know that the Chinese had been writing this way for thousands of years.

As he experimented, he began to understand how words come apart. He learned to recognize the same syllable in different words. He began to make a sign for each syllable, and within a month he could "spell" every word in the language. But he used two hundred letters, which he thought was still too complicated. He went over and over the syllables to discover their simplest forms. Finally he reduced the whole language to eighty-six syllables.

Now he worked on the shapes of the letters. From a newspaper picked up beside the road he borrowed a few English letters, giving them Cherokee sounds. He invented the others he needed. As he worked, his six-year-old daughter learned the names of the letters. In English the same *e* sounds differently in *peek, peck* and *perk*. But in Sequoyah's system, every letter said its own name whenever it appeared. When his daughter had learned the names of the letters, she could read.

Eighteen years after he boasted, "I can do it myself," Sequoyah showed his talking leaves to some of the Cherokee. They knew he was a queer man from a magician's clan who marked on wood and muttered strange sounds to himself, and so they shook their heads. As Sequoyah tried to explain he wrote "Turtle Fields," the name of one of the chiefs who was listening. Sequoyah's daughter looked over his shoulder and read it out loud.

Within three years thousands of Cherokee could read and write. A child could learn the eighty-six characters in two or three days. A young teacher named Atsee, a hunter's son who had gone to a white mission school, translated the gospel of St. John into Cherokee. In 1828 the Nation bought a printing press, with both English and Cherokee typefaces, to print the laws passed by the Cherokee Legislature and to publish a newspaper, the *Cherokee Phoenix and Indian's Advocate*. It reported the Worm's account of his trip to Mexico in 1842 with Sequoyah and his son, looking for a band of Cherokee. The Worm said they found the Mexican band not far from San Antonio, that Sequoyah died and they buried him down there.

The Worm didn't say why Sequoyah felt it was so important to find that Cherokee band. What Sequoyah says in this book is what I think might have been the truth.

Calvin is not a fact at all, but only as true as I could imagine him.